Raves For the Work of
DONALD E. WESTLAKE

D1545488

Betty Benson closed the door and turned to face me. "If you try anything," she said, "I can scream."

I sat on the studio couch.

"You wanted to talk about Mavis," she said.

"Uh huh."

"Tesselman sent you to look for whoever killed her?"

"Right again."

She shook her head. "It just doesn't seem like him," she said. "That dirty old man."

"Why do you say that?"

"Because that's what he is. He came here once and tried to seduce me. He knew I was Mavis's best friend. And he was old enough to be my grandfather."

"He's old enough to be Mavis's grandfather, too," I said.

"She thought he could help her in her career."

"Did you think so?"

"He could have," she said. "But I bet he wouldn't have. Mavis never learned. She kept going off and sleeping with men who promised her the moon, and they were all the same, all nothing but liars. But she never did learn. She was always sure that this was the time, this man was telling the truth."

"Tesselman wasn't the only one, then," I said. I had the notebook and pencil ready. "Who was next on the rich-man parade?"

"You make it sound a lot harsher than it was. Mavis wasn't a—a prostitute, or anything like that."

"I know. She was only mercenary."

"A lot of people are," she said...

The
CUTIE

by **Donald E. Westlake**

A HARD CASE CRIME NOVEL

A HARD CASE CRIME BOOK
(HCC-053)
March 2009

Published by

Dorchester Publishing Co., Inc.
200 Madison Avenue
New York, NY 10016

in collaboration with Winterfall LLC

*This book is a work of fiction. Names, characters, places, and
incidents either are the products of the author's imagination or
are used fictitiously, and any resemblance to actual events or
persons, living or dead, is entirely coincidental.*

ISBN 0-8439-6114-7
ISBN-13 978-0-8439-6114-0

Cover design by Cooley Design Lab

Typeset by Swordsmith Productions

The name "Hard Case Crime" and the Hard Case Crime logo
are trademarks of Winterfall LLC. Hard Case Crime books are
selected and edited by Charles Ardai.

Printed in the United States of America

Visit us on the web at www.HardCaseCrime.com

For Larry and Nedra

Chapter One

Ella and I went to bed at two-thirty. We turned off the light, reached for each other, and the doorbell rang.

I swore, and Ella's hand tightened on my shoulder. "Maybe they'll go away," she whispered.

The answer was another nervous jabbing at the bell. Whoever was outside was in a hurry. I sat up, switched on the table lamp beside the bed, and Ella and I squinted at one another. She was a good-looking woman, a damn good-looking woman. Black hair falling soft to her shoulders, lips full and red and bruised-looking, eyes half-closed and waiting. She was sitting up, leaning toward me, and the sheet had fallen away from her breasts. I didn't want to leave her, not now, not for anything. I didn't care who it was out there, Ed Ganolese or anybody.

The bell jangled again, and Ella smiled at me, to let me know she knew what I was thinking, and that she had the same thoughts. "Hurry back," she whispered.

"Two seconds," I told her. I pushed the sheet out of the way and climbed to my feet. While I was yanking on some clothes, the bell sounded again. I stomped through the apartment to the living room, ready to punch a face in.

Usually, when the bell rings, I check through the

peephole before opening the door, but this time I was too annoyed to be cautious. I pulled the door open and glared.

It was Billy-Billy Cantell, jittering like a Model T. I didn't say a word for a minute, I just stared at him. Of all the people I know, Billy-Billy Cantell is one of the last I'd think of as a possible two A.M. visitor. He's a scrawny, scraggy, scrubby little bum who might be thirty or forty or fifty, you can't tell from looking at him. He's one of the poor clowns for whom life is spelled with a capital H, and I do mean heroin. He does everything it is possible to do with narcotics. He buys it, sells it, transports it, and takes it. He's a retailer on the Lower East Side, and I hadn't seen him for six months or more. The last time we'd talked, it was because he owed Ed Ganolese some money and I'd asked Ed not to send one of the regular collectors. I talked to him about it myself, being careful not to break any bones, and he paid up a couple days later.

The point of all this is that Billy-Billy Cantell and I do not normally move in the same circles, and I wasn't used to the idea of him dragging me out of the sack at two-thirty in the morning. So I asked him what the hell he thought he was doing, and he blubbered at me. "Cuh-Clay," he started, "you guh-got to help me. I'm in a jah-juh-jam." See where he gets the name Billy-Billy?

"What's that to me?" I asked him. I wasn't worried about this little snowbird and his little problems. I was thinking about Ella, waiting for me three rooms away.

Billy-Billy was chattering and flinching, and his hands were jerking around, and he kept glancing in terror down toward the elevators. "Luh-let me in, Clay," he begged me. "Plea-please."

"You got law on your tail?"

"Nuh-no, Clay. I duh-don't think so."

He kept shaking like an IBM machine gone crazy. He looked as though he'd fall apart any second now, and there'd be pieces of him rolling all over the hall. I shrugged and stepped aside and said, "Come on in, then. But this better not take very long."

"It wuh-won't, Clay," he promised me. He scampered inside, and I shut the door after him. Even inside the apartment, he kept looking around and shaking, and I wondered whether I should offer him something to drink. I finally decided it wasn't worth it. Besides, alcohol isn't his vice.

I pointed at a chair. "Sit down," I told him. "And quit shaking. You're making me nervous just looking at you."

"Thu-thanks, Clay."

When we were both seated, I said, "All right. What is it?"

"I been pat-puh-patsied, Clay. S-s-s-somebody s-set me up for a bad-buh-bad rap."

"How'd they do this? From the beginning, Billy-Billy, and take it easy."

"I'll tuh-try, Clay," he said. And he really did try. You could see him struggling to get himself all into one piece. He almost made it. "I guh-got a little high this after-afternoon," he jabbered. "I muh-made s-s-s-some guh-good s-s-s-sales and give myself-myself a guh-good jolt. I wuh-went to s-s-s-sleep and wuh-woke up in this apart-apart-apartment. And there was this buh-broad there. S-s-s-somebody knifed her."

"You," I said.

He looked more terrified than ever. "Nuh-no, Clay. Honest. I duh-don't carry no blade. I ain't the ty-type."

"How do you know what you did while you were high?"

"All I duh-do is fuh-fall asleep. You can ask any-any-body."

"So this time you did something different."

"I duh-don't even know-know this buh-broad," he stammered. "I wouldn't kill-kill nobody, Clay."

I sighed. Ella was still waiting for me, and this— There was a pack of cigarettes on the end table near me. I shook one out, lit it, and said, "Okay. You didn't kill her."

"I knuh-know I didn't, Clay."

"Where was this place?"

"I duh-don't know. I just-just got out of there, as fuh-fast as I could."

"Anybody see you leave?"

"I duh-don't think so. Wuh-when I got duh-down to the corner, I s-s-s-saw a puh-prowl car puh-pull up in front of the puh-place. The guy who s-s-s-set me up musta-musta tipped them."

"You clean your fingerprints off the doorknob and everything before you left?"

"I wuh-was too shuh-shook, Clay. I even luh-left my huh-hat."

"Your hat?" I remembered that hat of his. It was a little plaid cap, like the one Humphrey Pennyworth wears in the Sunday funnies. But Humphrey's cap is too small for him, and Billy-Billy's is too big. It's a plaid, mainly red, and it droops down over his ears, and Billy-Billy, afraid maybe that he'd lose it while his head was still in it, has written his name and address inside, in indelible pencil.

"I'm in a juh-jam, Clay," he said.

"You're damn right you are. How'd you get into this place to begin with?"

"I duh-don't know. I juh-just fell asleep."

"Where?"

"Downtown s-s-somewhere. This place was uptown, nuh-near the puh-park. I couldn't of made-muh-made it all the wuh-way up there."

"No? You *did* make it all the way up there."

"Cuh-Clay, you got to huh-help me."

"Like what? What am I supposed to be able to do?"

"Cuh-call Ed Ganolese."

That one set me back. "You're nuts," I told him. "You're out of your head. You must still be high. It's almost three o'clock in the morning."

"Puh-please, Clay. He-he'd wuh-want you to cuh-call him."

"What do you expect Ed to do for you? If you really did leave your hat there, and fingerprints all over the place, you are now hot. Too hot for Ed or anybody else to touch. Ed can't get you out of this like it was a user rap."

"Puh-please, Clay. Just call him."

"Why not go see him yourself?"

"He tuh-told me not to cuh-come around. He duh-don't want his wuh-wife or kids to s-s-s-see me. That buh-bodyguard of his wuh-would throw me out. Buh-but you could cuh-call him and tuh-tell him what hap-happened."

"Why should I?"

"Juh-just s-s-s-see what he's guh-got to s-s-s-say, Clay, please."

I had a feeling I knew what Ed would have to say. If somebody had set Billy-Billy up to take a bum rap, he had done a fine job of it. A murder charge isn't all that easy to fix. And with somebody like Billy-Billy Cantell, it just isn't worth the effort.

Which doesn't mean that Ed would tell me to leave Billy-Billy for the cops. Far from it. Billy-Billy was, after all, a junkie, and he was also a member of the organization. He knew too much about the narcotics business, sources of supply, delivery points, names of retailers. Put him in a cell for twenty-four hours, and he would say anything about anybody. All the cops would have to do is promise him a needle.

So I had a feeling I knew what Ed would have to say when I filled him in on Billy-Billy's problem. It was standard operating procedure. I give Billy-Billy a fatal accident, and leave the remains for the cops. Then John Law is happy, because a case has been closed. And the organization is happy, because things are calm and peaceful again. And I'm happy, because I can go back to Ella. Everybody's happy but Billy-Billy, and he isn't worried about anything any more. So maybe he's happy, too.

That was standard operating procedure. But I didn't

think I should go ahead with it on my own authority. Billy-Billy had been talking as though there was something between him and Ed Ganolese that I didn't know about. Maybe it was nothing, probably it was nothing—what could Ed Ganolese and Billy-Billy Cantell have in common?—but there was no sense taking an unnecessary chance.

I got to my feet. "Okay," I said. "I'll call him. But he won't be happy about it."

"Thu-thanks, Clay," he said, and that scrubby little face broke out in a great big smile. "I rea-ruh-really appreci-a-a-appreciate this."

"You wait here," I told him. "I'll call from the bedroom. If you pick up the extension in here and try to listen in, I'll hear you. And I'll come in and take you apart."

"I wuh-wouldn't do that, Clay. Honest. You know-know me buh-better than that."

"Sure."

I walked back to the bedroom and grimaced at Ella. "Problems," I said.

"Very long?" she asked me.

She was sitting up in bed, a pillow fluffed up against the headboard behind her. She had the kind of face which is most beautiful with no make-up on at all. She had no make-up on now, and her lips were full and pale red, her eyes large and deep and hazel-colored, her skin warm-looking and tanned. Her face was framed by that soft black hair, deep as night in the glow from the table lamp. Her body, outlined beneath the sheet, was full and firm and curving, and I didn't want to call

Ed Ganolese or worry about Billy-Billy Cantell, all I wanted to do was crawl under that sheet beside that warm soft body—

I looked away from her and sat down on the edge of the bed. "A couple minutes more," I said. "I've got to call Ed."

"Do you want me to wait in the kitchen?" Ella was a smart woman, and a good woman to have around. I don't think she ever really approved of Ed Ganolese and my job, but she never said anything about it. She just ignored it, didn't want me to talk to her about anything I did, didn't want to hear anything about it at all. And she assumed that I wouldn't want her to know very much about my work, so she moved out of hearing range whenever I had to talk business with anyone.

But this time it didn't really matter. Billy-Billy had arrived, I would call Ed, he would tell me to do what I already knew I had to do, and that would be all there was to it. So I said, "It isn't important. You don't have to get up."

"Hurry," she said.

I was afraid to look at her. "I will," I said, and reached for the phone on the bedside table. I dialed Ed's home number, and waited for eight rings. Then Tony Chin, Ed's bodyguard, answered, and I told him who I was and that I wanted to talk to Ed. He grunted, and clanked the phone down on a table or something. I've never heard Tony Chin do anything else *but* grunt. If he knows how to talk, you can't prove it by me.

I waited a few minutes, and finally Ed came on the

line. "It's after three in the morning, Clay," he said. "This better be important."

"I'm not sure it is," I admitted. Then I filled him in, telling him what Billy-Billy had told me, and wound up by saying that Billy-Billy had begged me to call him.

"That's no good," he said thoughtfully. "You did right, calling me."

"Want me to give him an accident, Ed?"

I heard Ella make a quick sound behind me, and for a second I wished I'd told her to go to the kitchen after all. In the two weeks Ella'd been living with me, the fact that I was occasionally called on to give people accidents had been carefully ignored by both of us. I wasn't sure what her reaction would be.

But my worrying about Ella lasted only a second. Then Ed answered my question, with a loud and surprisingly vehement "No!" and I spent a couple of blank seconds trying to figure out what that meant.

Ed went on, "Get him out of the city. Right away. Take him up to Grandma's. When you get back, call me."

"Now, Ed?" I threw Ella a helpless look.

"Of course, now. You want to wait till the law shows up?"

"Ed," I said, "I've got something on the fire here—"

"Turn the fire off, put a cover on the pot, and get going. Call me when you get back to town."

"I don't get it, Ed. Billy-Billy isn't anybody. He isn't worth fifteen cents for parts."

"I'll give it to you in words of one syllable," he said. "Billy-Billy has friends across the big water. Somebody

he met over there during the war, somebody big. He
knows better than to try to use the in for anything,
because it isn't that strong. But it's strong enough to
make us help him out of this. The guy wouldn't like it
if he found out we'd thrown Billy-Billy to the wolves."

"We won't tell him," I suggested.

"Fine idea. Only trouble is, Joe Pistol's here."

"Who? I don't think I know the name."

"He just got off the boat, bringing greetings from all
our friends overseas. He hopes the New York branch
is doing well. He's what you might call an inspector."

"Oh," I said. Then I knew what Ed meant. Practically
every ounce of narcotics in the country is imported,
because it's a little too dangerous to try growing your
own in this country. That means that Ed has a close
tie-in with a couple of boys in Europe. He's the distributor for them just the way Billy-Billy is a distributor
for Ed. Every once in a while, a representative from
one of these European boys comes over and looks
around a little, not saying much of anything, just to see
how things are doing. If he should happen to decide
that things aren't doing as well as they might, there
would very likely be a shuffling of authority, and Ed
would no longer be my boss. And, since a new broom
sweeps clean, Ed and I would probably go together.

And into all this comes Billy-Billy, who did something non-dangerous behind the lines during World
War Two and who probably worked black market a bit.
He wasn't a snowbird then. He met somebody, did the
guy a favor or two, and it turns out that that somebody
became very big after the war, and still remembered

Billy-Billy. Which complicates things when standard operating procedure calls for Billy-Billy to have an accident.

"Get going, Clay," Ed told me. "Call me when you come back, and we'll figure out what to do next."

"Yeah, Ed," I said. "Sure."

He hung up, and I sat there holding the phone for a minute. "I'll be double-damned," I said.

"What's the matter?" Ella asked me.

I looked at her, then at the silent phone, and then back at her again. I put the phone back in its cradle, and said, "I've got to go to New Goddam England."

"Now?"

"I'll be a royal son of a bitch," I said.

"Now, Clay?"

"He's got friends. That two-bit, unwashed, flea-ridden, dime-a-dozen punk has friends." I got to my feet and glared at the phone. "Why?" I wanted to know. "Why should a lousy punk like that have friends? Why should I have to go all the way up to New England because that good-for-nothing bum has friends?"

I might have kept on that way for quite a while, but the doorbell rang again, cutting me off. "Oh, for Christ's sake," I said. "Another one."

I stormed on through the apartment, and met Billy-Billy coming the other way. We met in the hall between the dining room and the bedroom. He looked more terrified than ever. "Cops!" he whispered. "It muh-must be cops! Wuh-where can I hide?"

"You stay the hell out of the bedroom," I told him. I looked around. The bathroom was to the left, the combination den and hi-fi room to the right. "Go on in there," I told him, motioning at the den. "Come on, hurry."

He hurried, and I followed him in. Along one wall I have a waist-high bench, where the turntable, tape recorder, pre-amp and amplifier are all lined up. I use the space beneath this bench for storage, and I have sliding doors across in front of the storage space. I shoved one of the doors aside now, and prodded some junk back into a corner. "Crawl in there," I told him. "And stay there until I come looking for you."

"Thu-thanks, Clay," he said, and crawled into the space I'd made for him. He went head-first, and I had to work hard to resist the impulse to boot that bony butt of his a good one. But I was afraid I might drop-kick him into some expensive equipment, so I just waited until he was all the way inside, and then I slid the door shut in front of him.

My second visitor, whoever he was, was a lot more patient than Billy-Billy. He didn't ring for the second time until I was on my way out of the den. I called out, "Hold it a second!" and hurried through to the living room.

This time, I was more careful. I looked through the peephole to see who it was outside there, and I saw Billy-Billy had been right. There were three cops out there, one of whom I knew, a plainclothesman named Grimes, who worked out of a precinct on the Upper East Side. The other two, both of them strangers to me, were also in plainclothes, and they looked a lot like Grimes. Heavy, dour, stern faces. Baggy plain-pipe-rack suits. Broad shoulders and no waists. All of them in their late thirties or early forties, but already well into middle-aged spread.

I opened the door, opening it wide to keep from looking suspicious. "Mr. Grimes," I said. "Social call?"

"Not so's you'd notice," he told me. He pushed me away from the door and came into the apartment. I only had the one lamp on, over by the chair Billy-Billy had been sitting in, and Grimes glared around the semidark room for a minute until his sidekicks were inside and the door was closed, and then he turned to me. "Do you know a punk named Billy-Billy Cantell?"

"Sure. A junkie. Hangs out on the Lower East Side."

"When'd you see him last?"

"Tonight."

That surprised them. They hadn't expected me to admit that he'd been around. They'd been hoping to get me off-balance, in the cute manner of cops everywhere, but I'd been lucky enough to get them off-balance first. They looked at one another and back at me, and one of the strangers asked me, "Where was this you saw Cantell?"

"Right out in the hall, there," I said, nodding my head at the door. "About an hour ago. He came in with some wild H-dream about waking up in a high-class apartment with a murdered woman, and I told him to go get lost for himself."

"It wasn't an H-dream," said Grimes.

I moved my face around to register surprise. "It wasn't?"

"He killed a woman," said one of the strangers.

"Billy-Billy Cantell?" I laughed at him, just as though it had really been funny. "Billy-Billy doesn't have the strength to kill time," I told him.

"He didn't use his hands," said the cop. "He used a knife."

I shook my head, being serious now, wanting to help these poor guys. "Wrong boy," I said. "Billy-Billy doesn't carry a knife. He's always getting picked up on one bum rap or another, and he knows if the law found a knife on him, it would be a nice cheap conviction."

"He carried one tonight," said Grimes. "And he used it."

"Listen," I said, still being the helpful citizen trying to set the cops straight. "I thought Billy-Billy was just talking through his hypodermic needle, if you know what I mean, but maybe he was telling the truth. He told me somebody set him up to play patsy. Killed the woman, dumped Billy-Billy in the apartment, and took off. Billy-Billy was high on heroin and didn't even know he was being moved."

"Is that his story?" asked Grimes.

"As much as I heard of it," I said. "I got rid of him as fast as I could. It's pretty late at night to listen to some junkie's dreams."

"It's a cute story," said Grimes. "I'll get a real kick out of it when he tells it down at the station."

"Who knows?" I said. "Maybe it's the truth."

"Sure," said Grimes. He started looking around the living room again, as though he'd just lost a cigarette lighter or something. "We don't have a warrant," he told me, "but we'd like to take a look around your apartment. You got any complaints?"

"One," I said. "She's in the bedroom."

"We'll try not to disturb her," he said. He nodded to the other two, and they crossed the living room toward the hall leading to the rest of the apartment.

"Hold on," I said. "We didn't get that complaint of mine straightened out yet."

They stopped and looked at Grimes. He shrugged. "Check under the bed," he said. "That's probably where you'll find him."

"All right," I said. "I'll conduct the tour myself, personally."

"You'll wait right here," Grimes told me. "They can find their way around without any help from you."

"I don't want them going into the bedroom," I said.

"That's too bad, Clay."

"Listen, Grimes, you can give me a bad time the day you've got a charge against me. Until then, I'm a citizen just like anybody else. If those two clowns of yours go barging into that bedroom, you're going to regret it. I promise you."

Grimes is not a cop you threaten, and I know that as well as anybody, but this time I was sore. And he surprised me. He studied me for a minute, and then he said, "This one something special, Clay?"

"Very special," I told him.

"Any fire escape outside the bedroom window?"

"No."

"Where is the fire escape?"

"Off the den. And you can't get directly to the den from the bedroom. You have to go through the hall."

"Okay." He turned to the other two cops. "Knock on the bedroom door before you go in," he said. "Give her a chance to get dressed." He looked back at me. "Good enough?"

"All right," I said. "It'll have to do."

"It will that."

The other two cops left the room. I wondered if they'd look under the hi-fi set. If they did, Billy-Billy and I would be going down to the station together. I did my best to be nonchalant. "Do you want to sit down?" I asked Grimes. "Or don't you do that on duty."

"You sit down," he said.

So I sat down, in the chair by the phone. He sat across from me, leaning forward, his forearms resting on his knees, heavy hands dangling, his eyes glowering at me with dislike and distaste.

There are four kinds of cops, none of which I like. The first kind is the fanatic, the second kind is the honest-but-reasonable, the third kind is the bought, and the fourth kind is the rented. The fanatic is out to get you no matter what. The honest-but-reasonable is out to get you, but he'll listen if you've got something to say. The bought can be very useful, but I hate to have to rely on him, because I never know but what he'll turn out to be only rented. The rented cop is a bought cop who doesn't stay bought, and he's probably the most dangerous kind of all.

Grimes was a cop of the honest-but-reasonable

variety. He knew a lot about me, but he couldn't prove any of it, and he was willing to be quiet until he got some proof. He didn't know it, but a big chunk of proof was quivering away under the hi-fi set right now. I hoped he'd never find out. A fanatic can be dodged, because he doesn't think. An honest-but-reasonable is rugged, once he's got something on you.

We sat there, staring at each other, neither of us very happy about the other, and in our silence I could hear the two cops moving around in the back part of the apartment. After a while, I heard one of them knocking on the bedroom door, and then I heard him muttering something. I waited a couple more minutes, and then Ella came in, dressed in a terry cloth robe, holding the lapels closed at her throat. She blinked at me, doing a good imitation of somebody just roused from sleep, and said, "What's wrong, Clay? What's going on?"

"They're just looking for a friend of theirs," I said. "Nothing to worry about, ma'am, just routine, ma'am. Ask Mr. Grimes there, he'll tell you. Oh, by the way, Ella, this is Mr. Grimes. He's a policeman. Mr. Grimes, this is Ella. She's a dancer."

Grimes acknowledged the introduction with a self-conscious grunt. Grimes, I have the feeling, is not only honest, he's highly moral. I think he was embarrassed at this indication that Ella and I were sharing bed and board without benefit of clergy. He would rather know I was out killing somebody than that I was sleeping with a woman not my wife. Ella embarrassed him, and he didn't know what to say or where to look. He carefully kept from looking at her, though she was completely covered by the robe.

"I'm afraid I don't know Mr. Grimes' first name or rank, honey," I said, enjoying the opportunity to put the bum on the spot. "Maybe he'll tell you himself."

"Mr. Grimes will do," he mumbled.

"How do you do, Mr. Grimes?" said Ella politely. "What's wrong here?"

"It's just routine," he said, and then he flushed, obviously remembering I'd just used that line.

"They're looking for a guy named Cantell," I said to Ella. I looked back at Grimes. "Though he really isn't here. You guys are wasting a lot of time. You could be looking other places."

"We're not the only ones looking," he said.

"What are you looking for him for?" Ella asked him.

"They think he killed somebody," I told her.

Then the other two cops came back into the room and shook their heads at Grimes. Cops never talk to one another. They just nod or shake their heads or wave their arms or blow whistles. This chunk of sign language now, the shaking of heads, meant that neither one of them had thought to look into the storage space under the hi-fi set, and I wasn't yet on my way to jail. As soon as the law cleared away, I was on the road to New England, which was at least better than jail.

Grimes, with this diversion relieving him of his embarrassment, lumbered to his feet and glowered at me. "I wish you'd believed him," he said. "I wish you'd hidden him in here, so I could take the two of you downtown."

"Mr. Grimes," I said, as I stood up, "if I had known Billy-Billy was telling the truth, about being set up and a killing and all, I would have called the police right away. There's a dangerous killer running around loose."

"Right," said Grimes. "And his name is Cantell. If he comes back, maybe you ought to call me."

"You going to put a stake-out on the front door?" I asked him.

"I might."

"What about the alley in back?"

"Maybe."

"If he comes back," I said virtuously, "I'll call you right away. I'm an honest citizen."

"You're a citizen," he agreed sourly. "That's what makes it rough. We can't deport you anywhere."

I grinned. "You're a real joker, Mr. Grimes," I said.

"So are you." He jammed his hat on his head and turned to the door. The other two cops went with him, and I trailed along behind. I said ta-ta to the bulls, Grimes rumbled something I didn't quite catch, and I closed the door after them.

Ella had lit two cigarettes, and now she handed me one. "What happens now, Clay?" she asked me.

"Now I go to New England," I told her.

"Do you have to?"

"No choice, honey. I wish I didn't."

"Clay, did he kill somebody, really?"

"I doubt it. More likely, he was set up to take the rap."

She went over and sat down on the sofa, curling her legs under her. She looked troubled. "Clay," she said, her eyes serious on me, "you've killed people, haven't you?"

"Honey—"

"Given them accidents, like you said on the phone."

"Honey, I don't have time—"

"You would have given this—whatever his name is— you would have given him an accident, if that boss of yours had said to. Wouldn't you?"

"Honey, we can talk about this when I get back," I said. "I don't have time now." That was the truth, but it was also an excuse. I didn't like the way she was looking at me, or the questions she was asking me. I didn't want to lose Ella. She was the first woman I'd had in nine years that I didn't want to lose. I cursed Billy-Billy for bringing my job into my home.

"I've got to get going," I said. "We can talk when I get back. Okay?"

"All right, Clay," she said.

I wanted to say more, but there just wasn't time. I left her sitting there, and ran into the den to get Billy-Billy. I knew just how to get him out of the building. Up the fire escape and across a few roofs, down another fire escape, through a window, and we'd be on the third floor of the parking garage where I keep my Mercedes. It's a route I've taken once or twice before, when people I didn't want to see were waiting outside my door.

I went into the den and shoved the sliding door out of the way. I stared at empty space. Billy-Billy wasn't there. I looked around the room, in a daze, trying to figure out where the hell he could have gone to, and I noticed the window leading out to the fire escape. It was closed. I'd left the thing open a couple of inches. Billy-Billy must have heard us talking in the living room, knew the cops were going to search, and made it out the fire escape. He'd closed the window behind him, to discourage any cops from glancing outside.

I went over to the window, opened it all the way, and stuck my head out. The apartment is air conditioned, but outside there was an August heat wave going on, and it was like sticking my head into a bale of warm cotton. I looked up, then down, then to both sides, but I didn't see Billy-Billy. The little punk must have been scared out of his wits. He had taken off completely, and where he was by now was anybody's guess.

My nice, quiet, relaxing night had been shot to hell. I cursed when I slammed the window again, and I cursed all the way into the bedroom. Ella was there, back in bed again, sitting up the way she'd been before. "What's the matter now?" she asked me.

"He's gone," I said. "I've got to call Ed again."

I did, and Tony Chin answered, and we grunted at each other. Then Ed came on the line, and I told him what had happened. "Fine," he said. "You go get him. Find him and hide him somewhere. Meeting of the board at nine o'clock, in Clancy Marshall's office. You find Billy-Billy, stash him somewhere, and be at Clancy's office at nine. After the meeting, you can take him up to Grandma's."

"He's running scared, Ed," I told him. "God knows where he'll go next."

"He's got to go somewhere. You know him, you

know the people he knows. He'll go to somebody. Get him. And be at Clancy's at nine."

"Okay, Ed," I said. I hung up and grimaced at Ella. "I've got to go look for the punk," I told her. "You might as well go to sleep. This just isn't our night."

"Do you have to go right away?" she asked me. "Couldn't you stay here for a few minutes?" The troubled expression was gone from her face now, and she was smiling at me, letting me know everything was all right again.

"I guess I don't have to leave right this minute," I said. I could give the law waiting outside a chance to get lazy.

"Good."

I left half an hour later.

Chapter Two

Outside was the city, and it had halitosis. The air was hot and damp, and breathing was a conscious matter.

I thought about Grimes, and the boys he would probably have somewhere across the street, waiting for me to lead them to Billy-Billy Cantell. I was the only one moving on either sidewalk, and most of the windows across the way were dark, except for a couple of night owls on the upper floors. Cars were parked along both sides of the street, though they'd all be gone in a little over four hours, at eight in the morning, when the no-parking ban goes into effect. In daylight, most of these cars would be two or three different colors, pastels, pinks and blues and all the other nursery shades, but now, in the hot darkness of almost-four in the morning, they were all black. Even the chrome spattered all over them looked subdued.

There was one street light on this side, way down to my left, and one across the street, off to my right. Grimes' boys would probably be in one of the cars parked directly across the way, in the blackness just out of reach of both street lights.

My street, in the West 80's, is a one-way east. The parking garage where I keep my Mercedes is down at the western end of the block, with entrances both on my street and on Columbus Avenue. If a cop was planning to tail me, and he was in the middle of this block, aimed at Central Park, and I was to go out the Columbus Avenue way and head straight downtown, that cop would have to circle all the way around the block to get where I'd started from. It shouldn't be too tough to avoid being tailed.

I plodded down the street toward the garage, and as soon as I moved, the sweat broke out all over me. I could feel the drops gathering on my forehead, getting ready for the straight run down through my eyebrows and into my eyes. Under the charcoal grayness of my suit, my white shirt was already sticking to me, and my tie was a hunk of warm rope around my neck. It was too hot and muggy to move, or to think, or to go running out of an air-conditioned apartment and look all over New York for a two-bit hophead with friends.

An orange cab cruised by, the dim yellow vacancy light lit on its top, and it looked like a big, wide-mouth, toothy fish, mooching around in the seaweed at the ocean's floor. That was a nice cooling thought, and I clung to it for a minute, until I got a look at the cabby behind the wheel. He looked twice as hot as I felt, and my shirt, in sympathy with him, got a tighter grip on my back.

I walked into the garage office, and the Puerto Rican kid who works nights was sitting there behind the desk, reading a comic book. He grinned and nodded at me and went away, without having said a word, to get my car.

The office was hot and bright yellow. The kid had left the comic book open on the desk and I leafed through it while I waited for him to come back. The lettering in the balloons was all in Spanish, but you don't need the lettering to read a comic book. What was that the comic-book publisher was quoted as saying? "We are retooling for illiteracy." I flipped the pages over and looked at the pictures.

The Mercedes hummed down the ramp and the kid climbed out, looking happy. It didn't matter to him that he didn't own any of the cars in this building. Just so he got the chance to drive them up and down the ramps, he was happy. How many Puerto Rican kids get the opportunity to drive a Mercedes-Benz 190SL?

He climbed out of the car and held the door for me, grinning. "All set, mister," he said.

"Thanks." I got in behind the wheel, and he closed the door for me.

"Pretty late," he said, looking through the open window at me. "You goin' out of town?"

"Naw. I'll be back after a while."

"Okay."

We grinned at each other, and I pulled out onto Columbus Avenue. The Puerto Rican kid, I knew, was confused by me. So was the doorman at my apartment building. I look and dress like a rising young executive, age thirty-two, height six foot one, hair brown and cut short, face squarish but kind of post-collegiate-looking. I blend right in on Madison Avenue.

But I keep strange hours. Sometimes, I'm out of

town for a couple of weeks. Sometimes, I hang around
the apartment for days. I come and go at a schedule
even I can't figure out. And once or twice there have
been cops around, asking questions about me. The
doorman has never said a word to me about it, but the
Puerto Rican kid tries to pump me from time to time,
in a casual, offhand sort of way. It gives us something
to talk about while we hand my car back and forth.

Now, I drove down Columbus Avenue one block
and turned right. I went over to West End Avenue and
headed downtown. I'd kept a close watch in the rear-
view mirror, and when the car that had been behind
me on Columbus Avenue was still behind me on West
End, I knew I hadn't ditched the cops so readily after
all. They must have had two men on watch, in two
cars, with radio contact or something.

But it just might be a fluke, so I tested him. I turned
left at the next corner, back over to Columbus, turned
right, right again at the next cross street, and the son of
a bitch was still on my tail, half a block behind me.
When I got to West End Avenue again, I turned left
and waited to be stopped by a traffic light.

It happened, finally, and I stopped well back from
the intersection. Way down ahead of me, I could see
the gliding lights of cruising taxis, but the tail and I
were the only ones motorized in the immediate neighborhood. The tail was driving a black '56 Chevy, which
figured. A cop will do a thing like that every time.
There are maybe twelve million cars in this country,
and ten million of them look like plastic toys from

Japan, all chrome and pink and yellow. So when a cop is trying to be inconspicuous, what does he drive? A black Chevy. With opposition like that, it's a wonder Ed Ganolese hasn't taken over the whole country.

This particular cop was even more inconspicuous than that. Instead of pulling up in the other lane beside me, the way any normal red-blooded licensed hot-rod would do, he waited out the traffic light behind me. And that's the way I got rid of him.

The light switched to green, and I slammed my foot on the accelerator. The Mercedes leaped out into the intersection like a panther diving off a branch, and then I stomped down on the brakes. The cop behind me, figuring we were in for a chase, had jammed his own accelerator to the floor, and the Chevy rumbled forward, just slightly out of control. Before he could get the foot over to the brake pedal, he'd rammed me.

I allowed myself the luxury of a grin, for just a second, then wiped it off, put an annoyed expression on my face instead, left the Mercedes in neutral, motor running, and climbed out of the car. I marched back and glared at my rear bumper, where the cop had dented it.

The cop, being a believer in the safety rules of the road, killed his engine and pulled on his emergency brake before he got out of the Chevy. I switched my glare to him and said, "Okay, buddy, who handles your insurance?"

He was a big, beefy type, dressed in the shapeless, baggy suit some manufacturer makes especially for plainclothesmen. "All right, you smart-aleck punk," he said, blustering because he couldn't figure out what I was up to.

"I hope for your sake you carry insurance," I told him. "It's compulsory in New York State now, you know."

He reached into his hip pocket, dragged out his wallet, and flipped it open to show me his badge. "You hit the brakes on purpose," he said.

"A cop!" I said, as though I was surprised. "And crowding me! Okay, friend, let's see the number on that badge."

"You can go to hell," he said.

"Foul language to a citizen," I said. I marched to the back of the Chevy, pulling pencil and notebook out of my inside jacket pocket, and copied down the license plate number.

"What the hell you think you're doin'?" he shouted. And he really didn't know.

He was still standing by the front end of the car, confused but belligerent. I walked back toward him, looking just as smug and righteous as I possibly could. The driver's-side door of the Chevy was open, and I casually closed it on the way by. I also casually pushed the lock button down as I was closing it.

I stood in front of the cop for a second and just grinned at him. Then I said, "I want to make this just as legal as possible. I've got a card from my insurance company in the glove compartment. Just a second, I'll get it for you."

"I don't want no goddamn card," he said.

"Still and all," I said. I brushed by him, climbed into the Mercedes, and slammed door, gearshift and accelerator all at the same time. I was three blocks away before the simple son of a bitch behind me even got his car door unlocked. I turned left, cut over across town to Second Avenue, and headed downtown to Billy-Billy Cantell's normal camping grounds.

Chapter Three

I knew there was no sense looking for Billy-Billy at home. He was smart enough to know that two-room cockroach farm of his would be swarming with cops by now. He'd go to somebody he knew, somebody he thought he could trust. And the most likely prospect was a guy named Junky Stein.

Junky Stein, like Billy-Billy, is a user-pusher, but there the similarity ends. Junky has managed to keep a nice lightweight monkey on his back, and he isn't a retailer. He's the middleman who supplies the retailers, after the stuff has been cut and capsuled higher up. Billy-Billy is one of his oldest and steadiest customers and I guess you could say he and Junky were close friends. Junky would let Billy-Billy ride on credit every once in a while, and the two of them often hit the needle trail to Nirvana together. If Billy-Billy needed a friend to hide him out, Junky would probably be the guy he'd head for.

Junky lived in a run-down fire hazard on East 6th Street, between Avenues C and D. I found a parking space half a block from the address, and climbed out of the Mercedes, wondering if I'd still have hubcaps when I got back. The Lower East Side is full of amateurs, who wouldn't recognize me or my car.

I walked along the filthy sidewalk, threading my

way through the garbage cans and the empty baby carriages and the drunks, and went up the steps and into Junky's building. He lived on the fourth floor and it was a walk-up. The stink in that place was almost thick enough to be seen, a bilious green-gray stench, and I breathed as little as possible as I went up the paper-littered stairs to the fourth floor. Cute sayings in a variety of languages were scrawled on the crumbling walls, and every apartment was pumping out its own individual perfume. There was no air conditioning in a rat's nest like this, and the heat was even worse in here than it was out on the street.

I made the fourth floor after a while, and knocked on Junky's door. There wasn't any answer, so I tried the knob. It turned, and the door opened in, and I went inside.

It was pitch black in there. I fumbled along the wall until I found the light switch, flicked it on, and shut the door behind me. There was Junky, sprawled out on the floor.

At first, I thought he was dead. I rolled him over on his back, and his mouth was open, and I could hear the air being forced in and out of his lungs. He'd pumped himself full of the stuff tonight, and looked good for hot storage all day long.

But I didn't have all day long. I poked him in the rib cage and said, "Junky. Junky, this is Clay."

He didn't move. He didn't even groan.

Normally, I let a guy alone when he's under like that. He paid hard cash for his little snooze, let him get his money's worth. But this time, I was in a hurry. So I poked him again, and said, "Junky. Dammit, Junky, wake up." I prodded him and slapped his face and pulled his hair, and he rolled his head back and forth, moaning and grumbling and fighting it all the way.

I heaved and shoved, and I finally got him standing on his feet. His eyes were still closed, and his head hung loose, but at least he was standing. I let him go and he swayed, but he didn't fall.

"Junky," I said. "This is Clay, Junky. Wake the hell up."

But he didn't wake up. He didn't know anybody named Junky. He didn't know anybody named Clay. He didn't know anybody.

"Okay, little man," I said. "Let's just wake you up."

I turned him around and walked him into the head. There wasn't a shower, but there was a tub, and I made him get into it. I helped him sit down, and he mumbled, "Thanks, buddy," and for just a second I felt sorry for the poor stupid clown, and I wanted to go away from there and look some place else and leave Junky Stein to his own private hell all alone. But he was still my best bet. Billy-Billy obviously wasn't here, but Junky might know where he was. So I put the plug in the drain and turned the cold water on.

By the time the tub was half full, he was beginning to come out of it. Just beginning to. He opened his eyes and he saw me, but he didn't recognize me. "What you doin' to me?" he wanted to know.

"Waking you up," I told him. "You want to get out of the tub now?"

"My shoes are ruined," he said.

"Sorry. But I couldn't wait around all day."

"You didn't have to ruin my shoes," he said. He still didn't recognize me.

I helped him out of the tub and went into the other room for some dry clothes for him. "Change into these," I said. "And come out sober."

He blinked at me, a thin, fortyish guy with strain lines on his forehead and around his mouth, shivering a little even though thermometers were blowing up all over the city. "Where were we last night?" he asked me.

"Heaven," I told him. "Hurry up and get changed."

I went back outside and closed the bathroom door behind me. There was a deck of cards scattered all over the table on the other side of the room, and I went over and played a hand of solitaire.

He came out after a while, dressed in dry pants and shirt, but barefoot. "What's going on?" he asked me.

"You know who I am?"

"I don't owe you any money, do I?"

I sighed. He was still way under. "Come on over and sit down," I said. "We'll play some gin rummy."

"I got a sour taste," he said.

"Come on, sit down."

So he sat down, and I dealt a gin rummy hand, and he picked up the cards and looked at them for a while. He blinked a couple of times, looked at the cards some more, put them down, looked around the room, looked at the cards again, and finally looked at me. "Clay," he said.

"Welcome home," I said.

"What the hell happened?"

"I woke you up. I'm sorry, Junky, but I had to."

"Woke me up?"

"When'd you go to sleep?"

"What time is it?"

I looked at my watch. "Quarter to five," I told him.

"Tuesday?"

"Uh huh. Tuesday."

"I came home about four."

"That when you took the shot?"

"Yeah. I guess so." He shook his head and winced, then pressed his palm against his forehead. "I got a hell of a headache," he said.

"I'm sorry I had to do it, boy. You can take another in just a minute."

"Jesus, my head hurts."

"Junky, listen to me for a minute."

He squinted at me from under his eyebrows. "What's wrong, Clay?"

"You see Billy-Billy tonight?"

"Yeah, sure. Around eight, at the movie over at Avenue B and Fourth Street."

"Not since then?"

"No. Why, what's with Billy-Billy?"

"What kind of shape was he in when you saw him?"

He managed a lopsided kind of grin. "The shape I was in when you saw me," he said. "Out of it. In the alley beside the movie."

"That was at eight o'clock?"

"Yeah. Why? What's wrong, Clay?"

"Billy-Billy got himself mixed up with a murder sometime after midnight."

"Billy-Billy?"

"He didn't come to see you an hour or two ago, did he?"

"I just got home at four o'clock, Clay."

"Okay. He's liable to come here anyway, pretty soon. If he does, you hold on to him, and call me. Right away. Okay?"

"Yeah, sure, Clay."

"If it's after nine o'clock, call me at Clancy Marshall's office."

"I'll be sleeping at nine o'clock, Clay."

"Yeah, I know. I'm sorry I had to wake you up."

"Hell, that's okay. I should of eaten something first anyway." He grimaced again, and rubbed his forehead some more. Then he stopped and said, "Billy-Billy's hot?"

"Right you are."

"How hot, Clay?"

"Very."

"Hot enough to be taken off the payroll, Clay? Because he's a friend of mine, you know that. I don't pull no Judas on him, I don't hold him here for you to come down and bump him. Get somebody else for that, Clay. Billy-Billy's my friend."

"Don't worry about it, Junky. You aren't his only friend. I got orders to keep him safe and get him out of town."

"How far out of town?"

"He isn't going to get killed," I said. I was getting annoyed. It wasn't up to Junky Stein to decide what was going to happen to Billy-Billy.

"Okay," he said. "If I see him, I'll hold on to him."

"Where else might he have gone? He's hot and he knows he's hot. He wants to hole up somewhere. Where would he go?"

"Beats me, Clay. Here, I guess. Or maybe he's trying to get out of town by himself."

"I doubt it. At least, I hope not. The law would get him for sure if he tried anything like that."

"I just don't know, Clay. He'd come here. I don't know anybody else he'd go to at all."

"None of his customers?"

"Hell, no." He prodded at his forehead with shaky fingers. "There was a place he used to go every once in a while," he said. "I don't know where, though. It wasn't a friend or anything like that, I don't think."

"What kind of place?"

"I don't know. He said he wasn't supposed to tell. He could only go there in the daytime, though, I know that much. He went there one night, and he came back without any money."

"Money?"

"He'd get money at this place, wherever it was. I thought for a while he was maybe selling blood to one of the hospitals, something like that, but he'd get different amounts. He wouldn't go very often, you know. Only if he was really in a bind for cash. Last time he went was a couple months ago, when you were down on him for some late payments. That's where he got the dough."

"You don't know where this place is, or anything about it?"

"I'm sorry, Clay. All he'd say was that he wasn't supposed to tell. Even if he was high, he'd keep a tight lip on that one thing."

"And there's no place else he'd go?"

"Not that I know of, Clay."

"Okay. Can you stay away from the needle for a while? Just to see if he shows up."

"My head hurts like hell, Clay."

"Try, will you? I've got to get that boy found."

"I don't promise nothing, Clay. Look." He held out his hands and let me watch them shake. "See?"

"Okay, I've got a better idea. You mind if somebody else stays here for a while?"

"Hell, no."

"Okay. Hold on."

I went over to the telephone and dialed a guy named Jack Eberhardt. He's mainly a muscle boy, but he could also be useful now, sitting around and waiting for Billy-Billy to show up. And he doesn't touch the needle.

He'd been asleep, but he said he'd be right down, once I'd explained what I wanted. I hung up, and turned back to Junky. "Did you hear?"

"Sure. I don't think I know the guy."

"Big," I said. "Black hair. Broken nose."

"Okay."

"Stay with it till he gets here, okay?"

"Okay, Clay."

"I'm sorry I had to wake you up."

"That's okay. Billy-Billy's a friend of mine."

"I'll see you around, Junky."

"Sure thing."

When I left, he was rubbing his forehead again, squinting at the face-down gin rummy hand.

Chapter Four

The hubcaps were still on the car, which was something of a surprise. I climbed in and sat there for a minute, thinking things out. Billy-Billy didn't have any other friends, except for Junky Stein and whoever the guy was in Europe. And maybe this money source Junky'd told me about. I'd have to see what I could find out about that.

He might have gone to one of his customers, but I doubted it. A pusher doesn't put himself in debt to a customer. It made sense for him to come to see Junky, and that was the only thing that made sense.

Unless the cops had him.

That was a cute thought. I hit the ignition, and drove back uptown. It was almost six o'clock, and rapidly becoming light. The streets had that tired gray look which is a combination of too late at night and too early in the morning. A few people were walking along the broad sidewalks of Third Avenue, looking worn and tired. Traffic was light, most of it cabs. It was six o'clock of a hot Tuesday morning in New York, and the only happy people were asleep.

I drove all the way up the long staggered-light stretch of Third Avenue to 86th Street, turned left, and went over and through Central Park, over to Columbus Avenue, and down to the parking garage.

The Puerto Rican kid was tired, but still grinning. "Gonna be a hot day," he said.

"Too hot to sleep," I said. This kid wouldn't have any air conditioning in his half a room.

His grin broadened. "I go downa 42nd Street," he said. "Thirty cents for the movies. Cooled by refrigeration."

"Shrewd boy."

"Thinkin' alla time," he said. "Maybe you could use a shrewd boy, huh?"

I shook my head. "Sorry, kid. I'm not the personnel manager."

"I drive like hell," he told me.

I got out of the car. "Don't let your boss hear you say that."

"You keep me in mind, okay?"

"Sure thing."

I left the garage and walked on down the block toward my building. I knew what the kid had in mind. Suits like mine, a hot car like mine, an apartment like mine, women like mine. He thought he could get the same thing, if he was in the organization. He didn't know he was better off where he was. I could get him a job, sure. Driving cigarettes to Canada and whiskey back, if he wanted to drive. Eighty a week and expenses, back and forth between Montreal and Washington, D.C., where you can get your cigarettes cheaper, without any state taxes to pay. Or maybe transporting narcotics up from Baltimore and Savannah. He was too light for a muscle job, too young for an important job, too Puerto Rican to get any advancement. Eighty a week and expenses, and the odds favoring him for a conviction and a jail term within two years. I could get him a job, if he really wanted. And he'd still sleep in the 42nd Street theaters during heat waves.

As I went into the building and headed for the elevator, I decided to let it ride this time. If he asked again, I'd set him up to talk to somebody. It isn't my job to recruit, but it isn't my job to turn recruits away, either.

The apartment was lovely and cool, and I just stood in the living room and breathed for a while. I was a little fuzzy in the head, from no sleep and too much heat, but the cool air helped a lot.

I went over to the telephone and called a cop, a precinct plainclothesman named Fred Maine. This was not a Grimes sort of cop. This was a bought sort of cop. I knew he worked an odd shift, getting off at four in the morning, which meant he should just be getting home now. He answered on the third ring. I told him who I was and that I wanted some information, and he said to hold on while he got a pencil. I held on.

He came back a minute later and said, "Shoot."

"A woman was stabbed tonight," I said. Then I glanced at the window. "Last night, I mean. In the living room of her apartment, somewhere near Central Park. The cops got to the place somewhere around two o'clock. They think they know who did it, but they're wrong. Can you get the story for me?"

"That isn't much to go on, Clay," he said doubtfully. "Women are getting stabbed in their living rooms all the time. It's like the common cold. But I'll see what I can do. Call you back in five minutes. You at home?"

"Uh huh."

"You want the name and address, right?"

"Right. I also want to know how the law got there so fast. And I'm also anxious to find out if they made an arrest yet or not."

"I'll call you back," he said. "Five minutes."

Actually, it was six minutes, during which time I lit a cigarette, loosened my tie and untied my shoelaces.

"This is Fred again," he said. "I told you it wasn't going to be easy. Between twelve midnight and three-thirty this morning, four women were knifed in four apartment living rooms in four sections of Manhattan."

"Great," I said. "The cops got any hot suspects for any of them?"

"Two. One on the Lower West Side, they got the husband for. The other one, Upper East, that's probably the one you want. They're looking for a pusher named Cantell."

"That's the one," I said. "They got him yet?"

"Not yet." He gave me the story. The dead woman's name was Mavis St. Paul, and the address was on East 63rd Street, near the park. Mavis St. Paul had been twenty-five, blond, five foot eight, and she listed her occupation as "model." She wasn't registered with any of the modeling agencies, at least not that the cops knew of. I could draw my own conclusions.

"This Cantell," said Fred. "He's a pusher and he's also a user. The theory is, he tried to burglarize her place and got panicky when she caught him at it. So he knifed her and ran. Left his hat behind, with his name and address in it."

"He's a smart boy," I said. "How did the cops manage to get to the place so fast?"

"Phone tip. Anonymous. You know, the solid citizen who's afraid he'll have to take a half-day off from work to be a witness."

"A phone tip, huh?" That sounded like my not-so-solid citizen, the guy who had left Billy-Billy behind to take his rap for him. Went to a phone booth, called the cops, and expected them to get there before Billy-Billy woke up. If they had, I wouldn't be awake right now, talking to bought cops.

"Let me know," I said, "if they get Cantell."

"Sure thing, Clay. And that shouldn't take long."

"What's that supposed to mean?"

"Homicide East is on the case," he told me. "Somebody upstairs is making a squawk about this one. It's hot."

"What the hell for?"

"Beats me, Clay. They don't tell me why, they just tell me do."

"Keep me posted," I said, and made another fast phone call, this one to Archie Freihofer, a fellow employee of Ed Ganolese's, party-girl division. He answered the phone at the sixth ring, and he came on sounding like butter. He always sounds like butter. I told him who I was, and said, "Does the name Mavis St. Paul ring any bells?"

A few seconds' silence, and he said, "Sorry. No. Should I know her?"

"Somebody must," I told him. "She lived on East 63rd. Occupation, model."

He snickered.

"Can you find out who paid the rent?" I asked him.

"I'll ask around. What was the name again?"

"Mavis St. Paul."

"Mavis?" He snickered again. "I'll look for a broad named Mildred who came from St. Paul."

"You can reach me at my place until nine," I told him. "After that, I'll be at Clancy Marshall's office."

"Okay, Clay."

"Work fast, will you? This is important."

"In three hours," he said, "I'll know where she has moles."

"Had," I corrected him. "She's dead. So be discreet."

"The essence," he said.

"Good boy." I hung up and pushed myself to my feet. I was getting more and more tired by the minute. I like my eight hours' sleep a night, and I was now one full night behind schedule.

I walked through the apartment to the bedroom, and I was surprised to see Ella awake, sitting up in bed and reading a book. "Why aren't you sleeping?" I asked her.

She closed the book and dropped it on the floor beside the bed. "I tried to," she said. "But I couldn't. So I tried to read, instead. But I couldn't do that either."

"What's wrong, Ella?" I asked her. But I knew already.

"I've been thinking, Clay," she said. And the expression on her face and the tone of her voice told me what she'd been thinking about. The "accident" business again.

"Wait till I get out of the coat and tie," I said, wanting to stall as long as I could. I hung my suit coat away in the closet, put the tie back in the rack on the closet door, pulled my shirt off and threw it into a corner, kicked my shoes under the dresser, and sat down on the edge of the bed. "It's hot outside," I said.

"Your forehead's all damp. Lie down here."

I lay back, my head in her lap, and she took a corner of the top sheet and rubbed it gently across my forehead, smoothing the perspiration away. "You look tired, Clay," she said.

"I am tired. But I can't go to sleep yet. I've got to be at that meeting at nine."

"How's this?" she asked me, and her fingers massaged my head, soft and gentle and soothing.

"That's fine," I said. I started to close my eyes, but I felt sleep coming on, so I pushed them open again.

We were both silent for a couple of minutes, as Ella massaged away the exhaustion and the tension, and then she said, "I want to talk to you, Clay. Seriously."

"All right," I said. I'd been trying to dodge it, but that was stupid. I knew we were going to have to go through this sooner or later, get it over and done with and behind us, once and for all. It might as well be now. Then I wouldn't have to worry about it any more.

"It's your job," she said.

"I know."

"Clay, don't get me wrong. It isn't that I'm shocked or anything, about you being a big bad crook or something stupid like that. It's just that—it's just the coldness you show sometimes, you—you're, I don't know, you're two different people sometimes."

"Don't be—"

"Clay. Don't tell me to don't be silly. I know, I know, you're fine with me, you're a nice guy and we have a good time together, but—then you can turn around and be so cold-blooded, talk about giving somebody an *accident* when what you really mean is you're going to go out and commit cold-blooded murder, and it's just as though it doesn't really mean a thing to you at all. There just isn't any feeling there, any emotion. And that scares me, Clay. With me, you show feeling. One of those two faces has to be false. I'm just scared it's the face you show me."

"You can't feel pity for a guy you're supposed to kill, Ella," I said. "Or you couldn't do it."

"Do you want to feel pity?"

"I can't. That's all there is to it, I can't. I don't dare to."

"You don't have to kill, Clay."

"I do what I'm told," I said. "I'm Ed's boy, he's my boss, he says do, I do."

"Why? Clay, you're smart, you don't have to be Ed's boy. You could be anybody's boy. You could even be your own boy, if you worked at it."

"I don't want to be my own boy."

"What's Ed to you, Clay?" she asked me.

I lay there through a long silence, my head in her lap, her fingers soothing on my temples. What was Ed to me? "All right," I said. "I'll tell you a story."

"A true story?"

"A true story. I went to college for three years, you know that, a jerkwater college in a jerkwater town upstate. Another guy and I, we were at this beer party, somebody bet us we couldn't steal a car. Crazy bet, ten dollars or something. We said we could. This other guy, he was a science major or something, he rebuilt his own cars from junkyards, stuff like that. We went out, we found this car, with an MD plate. That was the one for us. Cops don't stop an MD, no matter what he does. He might be on his way to an emergency. This guy crossed the wires, and we took off. We were both kind of high."

She interrupted me then. "What were you majoring in?" she asked me.

"How do I know?" I said, angry at her. "Business administration. I didn't know what I wanted to do. Let me tell the story, will you?"

"I'm sorry," she said.

"We took the car," I said. "It was wintertime, this is up in the Adirondacks, a lot of winter resorts, ski places and like that. This girl came running out. She wasn't a little kid, you know, she was twenty-something, a waitress at some lodge, she was running across the road because she was late for work. I was driving, I got all fouled up with the clutch and the brake and the

accelerator. I plowed right into her, then I found the
brakes. I clamped down on them, rigid, scared to
death, and the car went sliding. It was a Buick, one of
these big heavy jobs. It went off the road and hit a
tree. The guy with me went through the windshield,
got killed. The door on my side popped open and I
went out. Nobody saw it happen. It was wintertime,
you know, pretty late at night, cold as hell out. This car
was coming the other way, and they saw what happened, but they were the only ones. They stopped and
came over and one of them asked me what was wrong,
how did I feel? All I could say was, 'We stole the car,
we stole the car, we stole the car.' I could see my whole
life shot, right there. I should have known better, I was
twenty-three years old, two years in the Army, three
years in college. I should have known better."

"Was this Ed Ganolese?" she asked me. "The one
who saw the accident?"

"If you mean, did he decide to hold it over me, no,
you're wrong. These guys, three or four of them from
the car, they got my wallet, and I guess they saw my
student activity card. One of them said, 'A college kid.'
One of them leaned over me and said, 'Kid, you've
screwed up.' I don't know, I was shook up and scared
and groggy and still half-drunk. I saw one of them
wiping the steering wheel with a cloth, and the door
handles and the dashboard, and they helped me up
and into their car and drove me back to the college. By
then, I was pretty much sober, and not so groggy any
more. The guy in the back seat with me said, 'Kid, you

were lucky we came along. Go to bed and deny everything in the morning. They don't have a case on you.' "

"That was Ed Ganolese?"

"I didn't know it then," I said. "All I knew right then was that he'd saved me from a hell of a rough jam. He was on his way back to New York from wherever he'd been. I tried to thank him, but he wouldn't let me. 'I con the cops for fun, kid,' he told me. 'Besides, you don't need a rap like that. Go on in and go to bed.' So I did, and the next day, in the afternoon, a state trooper came for me, and they questioned me down at City Hall. A CID man. I told him I hadn't gone along with the bet, I was too drunk, I'd gone home and I didn't know what happened after that. They didn't believe me—they knew the other kid hadn't been driving, he went through the right-hand windshield—but they had to let me go, they didn't have any proof I was at the scene. I was scared, but I wouldn't change my story."

"So you got away with it," she said.

"Sure. The law couldn't touch me. But everybody knew I was there, or at least everybody thought they knew it, and that's the same thing. The people in school, I mean, the other students and the teachers. The students would cut me dead, and the teachers would give lectures on accepting responsibility, every class I was in. They wouldn't look at me in particular, but everybody knew what the lectures were all about."

"They were trying to help you, Clay," she said.

"Crap. Ed Ganolese helped me. He was the only

one in the world who helped me. Look, in the first place I was one of the crazy vets going to school on the GI Bill. This was a couple years after the Second World War vets all graduated, and a couple years before the Korean vets began to show up. A vet was an odd-ball when I was in school, there weren't that many of us. And we didn't have the money the teenagers had, going through on their parents' dough. They were ready to believe anything about a vet. They were down on him because he was older, poorer, and supposed to be wilder. So even though the law couldn't touch me on the hit-run, everybody on campus had me already tried and convicted."

"So you ran away?" she said.

"I tried to go back to school," I told her. "I tried to forget the whole thing, I'd had a close scrape and come up lucky. But nobody'd let it die. So I cut classes and packed up. I threw everything away I couldn't fit into one suitcase, a ratty old black thing with straps, you know the kind. Then I headed into town, for the bus depot. I didn't know where I was going, I was just going. I didn't want to go home. My father'd found out about it, and he didn't believe me either. I passed the hotel, and there was the same car, the guys who'd helped me that night. The car was right out front, with nobody in it. So I hung around for an hour, and then they finally came out and across the sidewalk to the car. I knew which one was the boss, it was easy to pick him out. I went up to him, dragging this damn suit-case, and said, 'Mister, I'm your boy.' He looked at me and grinned and said, 'What can you do?' I said, 'Anything you tell me to do.' "

She waited for me to go on, but I was finished. That was the story, and it was the first time I'd told it to anybody in over five years, and it made me nervous just to talk about it.

She said, "What happened after that?"

"Ed brought me back to New York with him. I drove cigarettes to Canada for a while. I was a New Look union boy for a while. I came up in the world. Ed knew I was his boy."

"Why, Clay?"

I closed my eyes. "Why? If Ed hadn't come along that night, where would I be today? In jail on a twenty-to-life for manslaughter and stealing a car and half a dozen other counts."

"It was a college prank," she said. "You might have gotten just a suspended sentence."

"The girl was dead, Ella. That doesn't come under the heading of college prank. Nobody else lifted a finger for me. Ed was the only one helped me. He saved me, so I was his boy. Besides, I hadn't known what I wanted to do. Nothing attracted me very much. Nine to five as a clerk or an accountant some place, I didn't go for that." I opened my eyes again, and looked at her. "I like this life, Ella," I said. "You've got to get used to that idea. You've got to believe it. I like this life."

"Which face is false, Clay?" she asked me.

"Neither one. Both. How the hell do I know? I've got

a feeling for you. If I let myself, I'd have a feeling for Billy-Billy Cantell, even if I had to give him an accident. But I can't let myself have any feelings there."

"You can turn your feelings off and on?"

"Not on, Ella. Only off."

This time, I was the one waiting for *her* to say something. Finally, I had to break the silence myself. "Will you stay?" I asked her.

"I don't know," she said.

Chapter Five

I left the apartment at eight-thirty, dead on my feet, and drove downtown to the building where Clancy Marshall, Ed Ganolese's lawyer, has his office. Ella still hadn't given me definite word one way or the other, and I worried about that all the way downtown. I didn't even think about the fact that neither Fred Maine nor Jack Eberhardt had called me with news about Billy-Billy Cantell. By now, one of them should have. A punk like Billy-Billy couldn't stay completely out of sight for very long. Either the cops would find him, or we would find him. One of us should have found him by now.

Clancy's office is on Fifth Avenue, and I knew it would be impossible to find a parking space anywhere in the vicinity. So I drove down Columbus Avenue until after it became Ninth Avenue, and turned left on 46th Street. I left the Mercedes at a parking lot on 46th Street, and took a cab the rest of the way. If I'd been fully awake when I left the apartment, I would have taken a cab right from there and not bothered about the Mercedes at all.

Sitting in the back seat of the cab as we inched our way crosstown, I thought about Ed Ganolese, and about what I'd told Ella of my first contact with Ed. In the garbled goulash of the newspaper trade, Ed Ganolese would undoubtedly be referred to either as a "crime czar" (in the tabloids) or a "syndicate chief" (in the kind you fold), but neither of those pat phrases gets the right idea across. I would call Ed the man with the finger in the pie. Any pie. Show me a pie and I'll show you Ed's finger.

You may never have heard of Ed Ganolese, but he is a very important guy in your life. At one time or another, he has probably bought a politician for you to vote for. If you ever came to New York for a convention and did things the little woman shouldn't know about, Ed probably wound up with some of your cash. If you ever guessed three numbers for money, Ed got a part of your dime. Likewise, if you have given money to horses or to other sports stars, or drunk much beer, or ever heated a spoonful of white powder over a candle while the hypo waited nervously in the wings, you have helped to make Ed Ganolese the wealthy and happy man he is today.

A man with so many varied interests obviously can't watch all of them at once. So Ed has people working for him, people whose job it is to stand on the edge of each pie plate and make sure nobody runs off with the filling.

But humans are, after all, only people, and Ed occasionally finds things amiss among his many pies. When that happens, he needs somebody to slap the kiddies who were naughty and to put all the filling back where it belongs. That's where I come in. Once, during one of those racket investigations that louse up the working day so badly, a reporter with a flair for the trite called me a "right-hand man and troubleshooter for crime czar Ed Ganolese." I'm neither. I'm a governess. My job is to keep the kiddies from annoying Papa and messing up the nursery.

Now, the cab finally made it to Fifth Avenue and to Clancy's building. I tossed a bill at the driver, climbed out, and hurried into the building. I was five minutes late.

I got into the elevator with a crowd of people on their way to work, and we started and stopped all the way up to the twenty-third floor, where Clancy Marshall, Attorney-at-Law, paid rent on three large rooms of office space. And practically all of this for only one client, Ed Ganolese. Clancy had a few minor clients outside the organization, of course, but only as a respectable cover. He made his living, and a good living at that, from the organization and Ed Ganolese.

I went down the hall to 2312, Clancy's office, and walked in. His secretary, a big, well-busted, well-hipped blonde with an I-know-what-you-want-and-it-will-cost-you expression perpetually on her face, was just getting settled behind her desk. She looked at me, recognized me, and said, "Mr. Marshall's expecting you. Go right in."

So I went right in. Clancy's office is all plush-carpet, gray-metal and bookcase-bound, and at the moment, there were four people present. Sitting behind Clancy's desk was Ed Ganolese, my boss. Ed looks as though he might have been a Latin lover in the movies maybe twenty years ago, but he's put on weight since then. His face is large and just slightly puffy, but somehow distinguished-looking in spite of that. His hair is still glossy black, though he's the other side of fifty-five. He goes to the right tailor and the right barber and the right manicurist, and he looks like a very successful and very shrewd businessman, the kind who automatically cheats on his taxes and marks prices up whenever there's nobody looking.

Sitting behind Ed, in the chair by the window overlooking Fifth Avenue, was Tony Chin, Ed's bodyguard. Tony Chin was undoubtedly born with a different last name, but I don't know it, and neither does anybody else, with the possible exception of Tony himself. And Tony Chin is a name that suits him. He's all chin and a yard wide. He's also two yards and four inches high. He isn't very bright, but he's pretty damn strong, and he's surprisingly fast. He's one of the best bodyguards in the business.

Clancy Marshall was the third member present, sitting on the sofa off to the right. Clancy is a tall, dapper, graying-at-the-temples, dignified shyster. He was dressed, as usual, in a severe dark-gray suit, and the narrowest tie ever seen off Madison Avenue. He was smiling as I walked in, giving out with that old barbecue charm, and I got that feeling about him again. That feeling is a conviction of mine that, if his parents hadn't sent him to law school, he'd have been a pickpocket instead.

Number four was a stranger to me, which meant he must be the Joe Pistol Ed had mentioned. He was sitting on the sofa, beside Clancy, and he was encased in a tight pin-stripe blue suit, the kind George Raft used to wear while scaring the kiddies at the Saturday matinée. This suit was double-breasted, wide-lapeled and shoulder-padded. It was also padded under the left armpit, which meant he was walking around begging to be picked up on a concealed-weapons charge. His face was one of those blanks, a blob of putty in the middle for a nose, eyes so small and so surrounded by scar tissue that you could barely see them, and a jaw almost as big as Tony Chin's. He was sitting there, waiting, absolutely expressionless.

Clancy gave me the big smile when I walked in. "You're late, keed," he said.

"I stopped off to push an old woman in a wheelchair down a flight of stairs," I told him.

He showed me his sparkly teeth. "Kidder," he said.

"What about Billy-Billy?" asked Ed.

"No word yet," I said. "I've got a guy waiting in Junky Stein's apartment. Junky's the guy Billy-Billy would normally go to. As far as I know, the cops haven't picked him up yet, and he hasn't showed up at Junky's yet."

"We don't want the cops to get to him at all." Ed pointed suddenly at George Raft. "I don't think you ever met Joe Pistol," he said. "Joe, this is Clay. My good right hand."

Joe and I shook good right hands, and he said, "Clay?" He said it with a rising inflection, smiling at me a bit, inviting me to tell him the rest of the name.

I smiled right back and said, "Joe Pistol?" I was inviting him to tell me his real name. He calls himself something stupid like Joe Pistol for the same reason Tony Chin has a new name and Clancy Marshall changed his name from whatever it was and I'm just Clay. A long time ago I was George Clayton. Today I'm only Clay.

"We want to get Billy-Billy fast," said Ed. "Clay, you spread the word wider. You don't know where a clown like that will run when he's spooked. Get onto everybody he knows."

I nodded. "Okay, Ed."

"I don't like this," he said. "It's going to screw things up. With Billy-Billy on the loose, the cops are going to be poking their dirty noses in all over the place."

"I got the word Homicide East is involved," I said. "Somebody higher up raised a squawk on this one."

"Why?" Ed demanded. "Now why the hell does it have to be like that?"

"I don't know," I said. "I'll maybe be able to tell you after I find out who Mavis St. Paul called sugar daddy."

Everybody looked blank. Ed echoed, "Mavis St. Paul?"

"That's the girl who got knifed," I explained. "I'm working on it now, to find out who she was playing house with."

Ed nodded and gave me a thin smile. "You've been working, Clay," he said. "Good boy."

Clancy chimed in, saying, "You look as though you didn't get much sleep, Clay."

"I didn't get any," I told him.

"I understand," said Joe Pistol, "this Cantell is hiding out somewhere?"

"We think so," Ed told him. "Maybe he's on a train,

for all we know. The cops don't have him, and we don't have him." He looked over at me. "By the way, Clay," he said. "You remember what we discussed last night on the phone, about Europe. You don't spread it, okay?"

I had to think for a second before I knew what he was talking about. Then I caught on. He didn't want anybody to know he had to go to bat for a punk like Billy-Billy Cantell because of somebody in Europe who's a bigger wheel even than Ed Ganolese. I avoided grinning. I could tell how the whole situation must be jabbing Ed in the pride. And Ed is a boy with a lot of pride. "I'll forget it all right now," I told him.

"Good."

Clancy spoke up again. "Even after we locate Cantell," he said, "we've still got a problem on our hands. The police will be looking for him. As you said, sticking their dirty noses in everywhere. We can't afford to cover for him, but we can't afford to turn him over to the police alive, either."

"We're covering for him," said Ed quietly.

Clancy was surprised. He knew standard operating procedure as well as I did. "Ed, I don't get it," he said. "The police will just keep looking until they find him. And they're liable to find a lot of other stuff first."

"Maybe not," said Ed. "A lot of killings never get solved. If the law doesn't find Billy-Billy, they'll just forget the whole thing after a while."

Even though I knew the situation better than Clancy did, I had to admit that Clancy had a point. "Ed," I said, "I don't like to butt in here. But you know as well as I do the cops only forget a case when they can't figure out who to put the grab on. This time, they've got a fine candidate for the grab, Billy-Billy. So they'll keep hunting, as Clancy says, until they find him. I'm not saying we should turn him over to the law, alive *or* dead. But we're going to have to do something to get the cops quiet."

"We're going to," he said. "We're going to do two things. First, we're going to get our hands on Billy-Billy Cantell, and we're going to get him out of sight, somewhere the law can't find him. Up in New England or somewhere. Second, we're going to have to find the cutie who set Billy-Billy up in the first place, and turn *him* over to the cops."

I stared at him. "You serious, Ed?"

"Do I look like I'm making a joke?"

"You want us to play Homicide Squad?"

"It doesn't make sense, Ed," said Clancy. "Cantell isn't worth it."

"Finding killers is up to the law," I said.

"The law isn't going to look any further than Cantell," he told me. "The cutie who set him up knows that. The only way to get the heat off Cantell is to turn it on the cutie."

"Ed," said Clancy. "Listen, Ed. How do we know Cantell didn't murder her himself? He was all doped up, he doesn't remember a thing. All this business about being framed and all the rest of it—that's only a theory."

"Have you ever seen Cantell?" Ed asked him.

Clancy shrugged. "I don't know. Probably. The name's familiar, I've probably bailed him out on user charges."

"Clay knows him. And he'll back me up on this. Cantell doesn't carry any armament of any kind, never did and never would."

"Besides which," I added, "he couldn't take a Central Park pigeon two falls out of three. No, Ed's right. Cantell was framed."

"And I want to know who set him up," finished Ed. He pointed at me. "That's your job." He looked back at Clancy again. "Your job," he said, "is to play lawyer. Get with those contacts of yours in the D.A.'s office. I want to know what the situation is, every step of the way. I want to know why Homicide East is called in on a simple slashing. If the time comes when Billy-Billy needs a lawyer, you're it. If they get him, you get him out. I don't want him in jail for a minute, not for a minute."

"Ed," I said. "About the guy who set Billy-Billy up."

"Find him."

"I don't know, Ed. He killed a woman named Mavis St. Paul. You don't know Mavis St. Paul, neither does Clancy, neither does Tony or Joe, neither do I. We don't have any kind of a tie-in with this woman at all. The guy who killed her went out on the sidewalk, grabbed a bum at random, dragged him into the apartment and left him there. The bum was one of our bums, and that's our only connection with the killing."

"You trying to say you couldn't find him?" Ed asked me.

"Hell, no, Ed, you know better than that. I can find him all right. But it'll take time. And meanwhile the cops are going to be agitating."

"Ed," said Clancy. "Listen, I don't think it matters whether Cantell is guilty or not. The police think he's guilty, and that's the important thing. I don't see why—"

Ed cut him off before he could get any further. "We don't turn him over to the law," he said. "Subject closed. Don't mention it any more."

"Okay, Ed," said Clancy. "I don't know why you're so set on rescuing this little nobody—"

"That's right, you don't."

All this time, Joe hadn't been saying a word. He'd just been sitting there, watching us all, interested but not particularly excited. Now, he said, in a soft voice. "They told me Americans like to talk a thing to death before they take any action. Now I believe it."

Ed gave him a sour look. "You're right," he said. "Meeting adjourned. Clay, go to work."

"Ed, wait a second," said Clancy. "I'm your lawyer, right? I tell you what to do to keep from having trouble with the law, right?"

"If you've got any suggestions besides leaving Billy-Billy Cantell for the cops, I'm all ears."

"All right. You don't want this Cantell to take the rap. Why not somebody else, then? We set up a fall guy of our own, get out from under that way."

"That would be a hell of a lot more complicated than getting the cutie who started all this," Ed told him. "Besides that, I want that cutie. Who the hell does he think he is, anyway? He can come around, grab one of my people, put the heat on the whole organization, and walk away whistling. The hell he can! I want him."

"Ed, you've got to look at this in a business way—"

The intercom on Clancy's desk buzzed then, breaking into the conversation, and Ed depressed the key. "What is it?" he said.

The secretary's voice said, "Call for Clay on one."

"Who is it?"

"Mr. Freihofer."

"I had him checking on Mavis St. Paul," I said. "I might as well take it, see what he got."

I walked over to the desk, sat on the corner of it, and picked up the phone. "Clay here," I said.

"Mary Komacki," he said. "Belleville, Illinois. Twenty-five years old. Been in New York six years."

"Hold it, hold it. Let me get pencil and paper."

"Okay."

I fumbled around Clancy's desk, got pencil and paper, and picked up the phone again. "You're talking about Mavis St. Paul," I said.

"Who else? Mavis St. Paul. Born Mary Komacki, in Belleville, Illinois, twenty-five years ago. Came to New York when she was nineteen. Went to acting classes for about a year, hoofed in a club, modeled a bit, got mixed up with Cy Grildquist for a while, two, three years ago."

I was writing like mad. "Cy what?" I asked him.

"Grildquist. The Broadway producer." He spelled the name, said, "She was trying to build an acting career on the casting couch. They were together maybe six months. Then Johnny Ricardo, who owns a couple of clubs around town. A few other guys."

"Who right now?"

"Ernest Tesselman. For almost a year. He's the boy who's been paying all that rent."

"I see. Anything else?"

"One more thing. Between boyfriends, she always roomed with a girl named Betty Benson. God knows what *her* real name is. She's been here five years and she's still at the acting-class stage."

"You got her address?"

"Yeah. Here, somewhere. Hold on."

I heard papers rustling, and then he gave me the address, on Grove Street in Greenwich Village. I thanked him and hung up, then read the name of Mavis St. Paul's boyfriend again. Ernest Tesselman. That explained why Homicide East was involved, and who was doing all the pushing from upstairs.

Ernest Tesselman is, to coin an understatement, in politics. He's never run for any office, never campaigned, never made any speeches, never addressed the graduating classes of any law schools, and never got his picture in the paper for making statements on national defense or atom-bomb tests. But he picks the boys who do. He and Ed Ganolese had been good friends for years, though they weren't partners or rivals or anything like that. But, like a brewer and a bottlemaker, their businesses were connected.

Tesselman, I knew, pulled a lot of weight around town. If someone were to stab his current baby doll, he would be very liable to put a bug in some official ear to get the guy, to get him fast and get him good. He'd be completely discreet about it, of course. The working stiffs like Grimes and Fred Maine would never hear a word from Tesselman himself. But one phone call to somebody way up in the stratosphere over the working stiffs, and pretty soon they would all be working extra hard.

Ed broke into my little reverie, saying, "Anything interesting?"

"Kind of. Mavis St. Paul belonged to Ernest Tesselman."

"Ah," he said. "That explains the interest."

"Doesn't it?"

Joe was looking politely curious. "Ernest Tesselman?" he said.

Ed explained who Ernest Tesselman was, and Joe nodded, then subsided into watchful silence again. Ed turned to me. "You'll have to go see him, Clay."

"Me? I don't even know the guy, Ed. What good would it do for me to go talk to him?"

"You're the only one who saw Billy-Billy Cantell after the killing. You're the only one who could convince Tesselman that Billy-Billy didn't bump his lady friend. Besides that, finding the cutie who really did bump her is your job, and maybe Tesselman can help you there, tell you who this whatever-her-name-was—"

"Mavis St. Paul," I said.

"Yeah, Mavis St. Paul. Maybe he can tell you who her friends were, who might have wanted to knock her off. I'll give him a call and tell him you're coming over to see him. Write down the address."

He gave me the address, and I wrote it down. "I don't know, Ed," I said. "This is public-relations stuff. I don't know this business."

"You just go talk to him," he said. "You just tell him the story."

"Tell him everything?"

"Of course. Give him the straight story. You won't get anywhere with him by being cute. What time should I tell him you'll be there?"

"Could I make it this afternoon sometime? I'm way behind in my sleep, Ed. I'm getting fuzzy around the edges. I'm afraid I won't be good for much of anything until I get some sleep."

"Okay. It's ten o'clock now, we'll make it for five this afternoon. You should be able to get five, six hours of sleep. Okay?"

"Sure, that's okay."

"You won't be getting much sleep until we get our hands on the cutie, Clay. Like they say in the Army, this is A-priority crash emergency disaster shazam."

"Sure, I know."

"Okay, meeting adjourned again. Joe, come on, let's go get some lunch. Clancy, make phone calls, get things set up. If the cops get their hands on Billy-Billy, you want to know about it right away, you want to get him sprung fast."

"Okay, Ed," said Clancy. He sounded doubtful.

"I'll see Tesselman at five," I said. "I'll call you afterwards, and let you know what he says."

We all left the office, all but Clancy, and rode down in the elevator to street-level. Ed offered me a lift, but

I vaguely remembered the Mercedes, over on 46th Street. I grabbed a cab, and sat back in it, fighting to keep from going to sleep.

I had to fight even harder once I was in the Mercedes, doing my own driving. But I made it to the garage, handed the car over to the day kid, who doesn't talk at all, and walked down the block to my building.

There was a cream-and-gray Ford parked out front, right next to the sign that says TOW-AWAY ZONE. The sun visor on the driver's side was down, and I could see the police sticker attached to it. I had a feeling I knew whom the little blue men were visiting.

Chapter Six

I was right. I walked into my living room, and it was full of cops. It looked like a whole convention of them. Grimes was back, and both of his buddies from last night, plus two more, both of them strangers to me. They were sitting around on the furniture, looking baggy and broad, like a bunch of used-car salesmen waiting for a victim. Ella wasn't in sight.

They all brightened up a bit when I walked in. I was the victim they'd been waiting for. "Ah," said Grimes, getting to his feet. "The prodigal returns."

"Sorry," I said. "I forgot all about inviting you guys over. Which kind of warrant don't you have this time?"

"Where've you been?" Grimes asked me.

"Out on Staten Island, distributing CARE packages to the natives."

"Very cute. Now we'll take it again for the real thing. Where've you been?"

"At the supermarket."

"Do you want to answer here?" asked one of the other cops. "Or would you rather answer down at the station?"

"What would you be pulling me in for?" I asked him.

"I wasn't going to mention that business about leaving the scene of an accident," said Grimes.

I winced. I'd forgotten all about that. I'd intended

to call the insurance company at eight o'clock, when they opened, which would have cleared me, but I'd been so tired, and was thinking of so many other things, I'd completely forgotten it.

Grimes grinned at me, so I guess I was too tired to keep a poker face. "Like to tell us where you've been?" he asked me.

"Mind if I make a phone call before you arrest me?"

"To Clancy Marshall?" Grimes shook his head. "We do mind, yes. You haven't been booked. And you won't be. We might hold you forever, but we'd never book you. We're just holding you for questioning. That shyster of yours would never find you."

"You'd see the inside of every precinct in Manhattan," said one of the other cops.

"And maybe some in the Bronx," said Grimes.

"No, thanks," I said. "I made that circuit once. Very dull. All those precincts look alike, every one of them. Green. Every wall in every station all over the world. Green. No wonder cops have such lousy dispositions."

"Where did you go last night, Clay, after you saw us?"

"To a vomitorium."

"All right. Let's go for a ride."

I didn't want to make that precinct circuit, I really didn't. "Look, Mr. Grimes," I said. "I'm tired. I haven't slept in four years. Come ask me questions this afternoon, will you?"

"Only one question," said Grimes. "And I'd rather ask it now. This is the last time I ask it, and if you give me a funny answer, we're going for a ride. Where've you been since I last saw you?"

"I can't tell you," I said. "I'd like to, I really would. I'd tell you anything, just to get some peace and quiet, so I can go to sleep for a change. But I can't."

"Why not?" asked one of the other cops.

"If I don't tell you," I said, "you arrest me, and we play precinct-go-round. If I do tell you, worse things happen." I turned back to Grimes. "I take it this has something to do with Cantell."

"You take it right."

"Okay, then, you don't need to know where I was. It didn't have anything to do with Billy-Billy Cantell, and that's the truth. Don't give me a rough time, will you?"

"Where did you go, Clay?"

I played it to the hilt. I gnawed on my lower lip, flashed a worried look at the other cops, shuffled my feet around, and finally said, "A meeting. A reorganizational meeting. I'll never tell you where, or who else was present, or what was being reorganized, or why. It had nothing to do with Billy-Billy Cantell, that's all I'll tell you about it. Billy-Billy Cantell is a two-bit, second-rate punk, and it would be a rare and strange day when anybody I know would go out on a limb for him. Be sensible, Grimes."

One of the other cops said, "Was Joe Pistol there? At this meeting?"

"The guy from Europe?"

"Probably."

"George Raft type," I said, "without the nose. I just met him."

"That's him," said the cop. "Was he the one doing the reorganizing?"

"No. He was an observer, that's all."

Another cop said, "This meeting didn't have anything to do with Cantell?"

"Of course not," I said. "Who's worried about a little bum like Billy-Billy Cantell?"

"I am," said Grimes. "I'm worried a lot about that little bum. I want him. And I'll play 'precinct, precinct, who's got the precinct' with you until you're eligible for Social Security if I don't get him."

"Why?" I asked him. "All right, all right, he got himself into trouble with a knife. But that's his business, his own private business. None of the rest of us are involved in it at all. Why should we cover for him?"

"That's what I want to know," said Grimes. "We should have had him hours ago. Somebody's hiding him. He's one of Ed Ganolese's stooges, so it figures that Ganolese or one of his other stooges is doing the hiding."

"You give Billy-Billy a lot more importance than we do," I said, and while I was saying it I was wishing it were true.

"What was Jack Eberhardt doing in Junky Stein's apartment?" one of the other cops asked me.

I blinked at him. "Who?"

"Come on, you know them both."

"Jack Eberhardt and Junky Stein? Sure I know them. So what? What's this got to do with anything?"

"Eberhardt was waiting in Stein's apartment. What was he waiting for?"

"How would I know?" I said. And I was trying to figure out what had happened. The cops must have figured Junky as a good contact for Billy-Billy, too, and when they went to his place they found Jack Eberhardt there. I knew I didn't have to worry about Jack doing any extraneous talking, but with Junky under again, I wasn't sure about him at all.

"He was waiting for Billy-Billy Cantell," said the cop.

"He was?"

"You know it as well as I do. What else would he be doing there?"

"Maybe he and Junky are friends," I said.

"You were out twice," said Grimes, changing the subject again. "Once between three and five. Then you came back here and left again at eight-thirty. Which time was the reorganizational meeting?"

"Both," I said. I wished I didn't have to spend so much time thinking. I was too tired to think, I had trouble remembering what I'd already said. "The first time," I told Grimes, "was just to meet this Joe Whosis, fill him in on the problems."

"You mean the problem of Billy-Billy Cantell?"

"No. I told you, this didn't have anything to do with Cantell."

"Just a coincidence, is that it?"

"That I was working? I wouldn't say that. I work almost every day."

"You're a glib son of a bitch," said Grimes.

Ella walked in, then, carrying a tray. She smiled brightly at me, the innocent little girl at a party. "Hi, Clay," she said. "I made some iced tea." She offered the tray around at the cops.

They didn't know what to do. A cop is ready for any situation except one. He doesn't know what the hell to do when somebody treats him like a normal human being, like a guest.

"We, uh, we don't have time," said Grimes uncertainly. "We were just leaving."

"Oh." Ella pouted a little, looking beautiful. "And I made all this iced tea."

"Stay awhile," I said. All of a sudden, I was enjoying myself. "You've got five minutes to drink some tea. It's hot outside."

They looked helplessly at one another, and finally they decided to stay and drink some iced tea. I'd been standing all this time, but now I sat down in the chair by the phone. Ella distributed the tea, and then sat on the floor beside my chair. She rested an arm on my knees and looked sweet and domestic.

There was an awkward silence, and I finally broke it. "I understand Homicide East is involved with this one," I said.

"We are," said one of the new cops.

"How's that?" I asked him. "I didn't figure Billy-Billy Cantell was important enough. Or was it the woman?" I'd almost mentioned her name, which would have been a mistake.

"I don't think you ought to worry about police business," said Grimes.

"It's just that Billy-Billy Cantell isn't very important to us," I told him. "I'm surprised to see how important he is to you."

"Sure," said Grimes. "I want you to pass some information on to Ed Ganolese."

"Sure, if I see him."

"You'll see him. And when you see him, you tell him we want Billy-Billy Cantell. We want him by tonight. We don't care whether he's still breathing or not, but we want him. And if we don't get him, we'll do some reorganizing ourselves. You tell him that."

"If I see him," I said.

"You want to be less cute," said one of the new cops. "You want to be one hell of a lot less cute."

"He can't help it," said Grimes. "It's his personality. He's a penny-ante crook with half an education, half a conscience, and half a mind."

Grimes could get under my skin every once in a while, and this was one of those times. "Mr. Grimes," I said. "Tell me. What's a crook?"

"You should know."

"I would say that a crook is somebody who breaks the law. Is that what you would say?"

"That's what I would say."

"So show me the man who isn't a crook, Mr. Grimes," I said. "Show me an honest man, Mr. Diogenes Grimes."

"Me," he said.

"You never cheated a little bit on your income tax?" I asked him. Ella looked up at me, squeezing my knee, warning me to stop, but I was too tired and too annoyed. "You never drove a mile or two over the speed limit? You never asked a buddy in politics to see what he could do about cutting your property assessment?"

He shook his head. "Never."

"Clay," said Ella softly.

"Just a minute," I said to her. To Grimes, I said, "You never looked the other way when somebody with influence skated a little too close to the edge of the law? You never listened to word from higher up to throw away a traffic ticket or remove the record of some rich man's idiot son's having been booked for drunk and disorderly? You never stood by with your eyes shut while graft money changed hands?"

"Clay, don't," said Ella.

Grimes was on his feet now, the glass of iced tea put down on a drum table. "You should have stopped talking a few sentences back," he said. "There are things I have to do that I don't have any choice over. And I don't like to be reminded of them."

"You're a crook, Grimes," I said. "You're a crook, just like me, just like everybody else in this world. There isn't a man alive who isn't a crook, and who hasn't always been a crook, and who won't always be a crook. But I'm just a bit more honest than most of you. I admit I'm a crook."

"Do you really think you can justify yourself?" one of the other cops asked me.

I looked at him. "Show me somebody I have to justify myself to."

"Okay," said Grimes. "Let's go. Let's go for a ride."

I shrugged and got to my feet. I carefully avoided looking at Ella, sitting on the floor beside me, looking up at us all. "Sure," I said. "I'll go for a ride with you.

And when you refuse me the phone call the law allows me, and when you keep me moving from precinct to precinct, ahead of my lawyer, you'll be breaking the law all over again. You'll be a crook all over again."

He grimaced and made a disgusted sound, as though he'd just tasted something rotten. "Stay here," he said. "Stay here, you smart boy, and kid yourself. But just be sure to tell Ed Ganolese what I told you. Produce Billy-Billy Cantell by tonight. Produce him, or you'll see just how crooked I can be."

"I'll tell him," I said. "When I see him."

"You do that."

Grimes led the way, and the five of them marched out of the apartment. I stood looking at the closed door.

Ella stood up beside me. "You didn't have to do that, Clay," she said. "You didn't have to antagonize him."

"He got under my skin," I said. "Besides, I've been antagonizing Mr. Grimes for years. It's a game we play. The funny part of it is, he *is* an honest man. And there is nothing in this world more vulnerable than an honest man."

She was studying me in a way I didn't much care for. "You aren't vulnerable, are you, Clay?" she asked me.

"I try not to be."

She stood looking at me for a minute longer, and I waited, wondering what decision was being made behind those level eyes of hers. Then she looked away from me, and crossed the room to where she'd left the tray. She picked it up and went to work, gathering up the glasses of iced tea.

I watched her, and I felt the heaviness and the weariness pressing down on me. It was no time to try to think, to try to talk to this woman. "I've got to get some sleep, Ella," I said. "I'll be okay when I wake up."

"All right," she said.

"Wake me at four, will you?"

"I will," she said. But she didn't look at me.

Chapter Seven

I was on board this gray ship, surrounded by fog, and an alarm bell was ringing. I was standing on deck, the wet railing on one side of me and a metal wall punctured with portholes on the other, and Ella was saying, "It's all glue," and somewhere the alarm bell was ringing.

Then the alarm bell stopped and Ella said again, "It's all glue." The fog pressed in tighter, and I thought, "I've got to get off this damn ship!" I opened my eyes and sat up and there was Ella. "Where's the lifeboat?" I asked her.

She looked blank. "What?"

Something was wrong, but I couldn't figure out what. We had to get to the lifeboat. Then I saw that Ella was holding the telephone out to me, and I woke up. I realized what the alarm bell had been, and this time Ella said, "It's for you."

"Thanks," I said, I took the phone from her, and glanced at the bedside clock. It was just a little after one. I'd only been asleep a little more than two hours.

I put the phone up to my face and said, "Clay here."

"Ed, Clay." He sounded annoyed and impatient. "You better get up to see Tesselman right now."

"What's wrong?" I asked him.

"The cops are going out of their goddam minds," he said. "That's what's wrong. They pulled two raids on collection points, one uptown and one downtown. Picked up over forty grand of heroin and a whole batch of pot."

"What for?" I asked him. I was only just barely awake.

"They want Cantell," he said. "There's been a general call. They're dragging people in by the dozens. Clancy's going nuts trying to get them all sprung again. And Archie Freihofer is tearing out his last six hairs. Half of his girls have been picked up, and the others are afraid to answer the phone."

"All this over Billy-Billy Cantell?"

"No, all this over Mavis St. Paul. Because she was Tesselman's."

"Ed, Grimes was waiting for me when I got home this morning."

"Grimes? Who's Grimes?"

"A cop. I've run into him before. He's working on this job. He told me he was giving us till tonight to cough up Billy-Billy, and then he'd start making life rough for everybody."

"Well, somebody jumped the gun. They're making life rough right now. So far today, they've cost me damn near a hundred thousand dollars."

"Grimes said we had till tonight, Ed."

"I don't care what Grimes said! I'm telling you what the lousy cops are *doing*."

"Okay, Ed, okay."

"And let me tell you something. Joe isn't happy. He isn't happy at all."

"Joe?"

"The guy from Europe. Are you awake?"

"Not really."

"Well, get awake. Joe doesn't like the way this thing is going. You know what that means?"

"Yeah, Ed. Sure."

"You go on up to see Tesselman right now. I told him you were coming. I'll call him again and tell him you're on your way. You go tell him to call off the goddam dogs."

"All right, Ed," I said.

"And find out who the hell started this whole thing."

"All right, Ed."

"I want that son of a bitch. I want that cutie nailed to a wall."

"Me, too, Ed."

Chapter Eight

Ernest Tesselman lived way the hell out on Long Island. It took a long while to get to the right neighborhood, and an even longer while to find his house. I asked directions a few times, but nobody knew anything. I finally got a sensible answer from a kid playing with a top. He told me how to get to Mr. Tesselman's house, and he was right.

The house, when I eventually did get to see it, was at one and the same time both impressive and a little awkward. You looked at it, and you knew the people inside had money. But you also knew they didn't have much taste.

The house was set back from the road, hidden by rigidly pruned hedges and heavily leafed trees. A black-top drive curved in a U-shape up to the front door of the house and back to the ornamental stone gate posts at the entrance from the road. The house itself was red brick, two stories high, and had four white columns marching across the front. The front door was white, with a phony brass knocker centered on it. Ernest Tesselman's land fell away on all sides, dotted with trees and bushes and hedges. Nary a neighbor could be seen.

I drove the Mercedes in and parked midway around the U, by the front door. I got out, walked around the car, and up the two steps to the pseudo-Southern-plantation veranda.

The brass knocker, as I said, was strictly ornamental and nonfunctional. A gold and white doorbell was to the left of the door. I pushed it, and heard chimes inside, playing something I didn't recognize. After a minute, a butler opened the door for me. He was decked out in a tuxedo and a supercilious expression. This was the type of butler who also doubles as a bouncer, and the tux didn't quite fit him. He bulged inside it, particularly under the arm, the same kind of bulge Joe Pistol had been wearing.

Fortunately, I don't have a face to go with my profession. No movie director would ever cast me as a "right-hand man and troubleshooter for crime czar Ed Ganolese," to quote that idiot reporter again. I'm more the insurance-salesman type, and I have no bulges under my coat. I never carry a gun on my person. It's the cheap way to a fast conviction. I have a Smith & Wesson .32 hooked under the dashboard of the Mercedes, with all the proper licenses and signatures, and I very rarely touch it, except to leave it at the apartment while I'm having the car washed. I don't want any car-wash flunky starting a new career with my gun.

I told my friend with the undersized tux who I was and that Ernest Tesselman was expecting me, and he let me into the house without a whimper. I got a quick glimpse at a living room done in *Life*-magazine contemporary, all tubular steel furniture and a hoked-up mantelpiece, and then Tux ushered me by and into a small room off to the right. He asked me, please, to wait a minute, and then he went away.

This room had been, in a previous reincarnation, a wealthy doctor's waiting room. Bookcases, ashtray stands, leather armchairs, coffee tables piled with old magazines, the works. I read the movie reviews in an old issue of *Time*, leafed through a copy of the *Post* looking for a funny cartoon, and then Tux came back. He asked me if I would come this way, and I said I would.

I followed him up a broad flight of stairs straight out of *Gone with the Wind*, and down a hall fresh from an old horror movie. It looked as though architects and interior decorators had worked on this place in relays, and no two of them were working from the same plans. A house like this would make me very nervous after a while.

Ernest Tesselman was in the last room on the right, down at the end of the hall. It was a large room, with lots of windows and a skylight, and was almost painfully bright. It looked like a supermarket for fish. There were straight rows of benches lined across the room, with narrow aisles between the rows. The benches were covered with aquariums, all of them filled with water and fish. Most of the aquariums had lights in or on or under them, and they all had filters attached at one end. The filters were all going *bubble-bubble,* most of the light sources were under water, I was surrounded by glass in the windows and the aquariums and the skylight, and the total effect was a little overpowering. I felt as though I were underwater myself.

I blinked a couple of times, trying to get used to the place, as Tux receded softly down the hall. Then I saw somebody swimming toward me down one of the aisles, holding a midget butterfly net in one hand and a box of fish food in the other. He was pausing now and again to cluck at the fish.

This was my first meeting with Ernest Tesselman, and he wasn't at all what I'd been expecting. I'd figured Tesselman to be somebody from the same approximate mold as my boss, tough and hard but lightly covered by a shiny veneer of social grace and civilized manners.

But this Tesselman was something else entirely. He was a little guy, gray-haired, with a small round pot belly, wire-framed spectacles, and bony hands on which the veins stood out like mounds of blue clay. He was dressed in scuffed brown bedroom slippers, faded and baggy-kneed corduroy trousers, a too-large undershirt, and a ratty white terry-cloth robe loosely tied around his middle.

I stood in the doorway, watching this fussy little Professor of Latin Literature scuffle up and down aisles and peek through his spectacles at the fish, and I waited for him to notice that he wasn't alone with the gills any more.

He did, finally. He blinked at me over his glasses, and said, "Are you the man Ed Ganolese called me about?"

"Yes, sir."

"Come in," he said. He waved the butterfly net at me. "Come in, come in."

I walked down the aisle toward him. By the time I'd reached him, he'd forgotten me again. He was peering into one of the smaller aquariums. All of the occupants of all of the tanks in the room were tiny, the things that are called tropical fish, and there was only one of them in this particular tank. This one was a sort of hazel color, with a red tail. It darted around, back and forth, as though it were looking for the exit and had just about lost its patience.

Tesselman tapped on the glass side of the tank with his fingernail, and the fish shot over to investigate the noise. Tesselman chuckled, a wheezy little sound, and looked up at me. "She's going to have babies soon," he said. "Sometime today."

"She's a good-looking fish," I said. I felt as though a compliment of some kind was called for, and what do you say about a fish?

"I have to watch her," he confided. "If I don't move the babies as soon as they're born, she'll eat them."

"There's Momism for you," I said.

"They're all cannibals," he said. He waved the midget butterfly net around at the rest of the room. "All of them. It's a very fierce world they live in. I want to save these babies. The mother is a red-tail guppy and the father is a lyre-tail guppy. They should have beautiful children."

I looked around at some of the other tanks. Most of

them had five to ten fish swimming around inside, and it looked as though they were all chasing one another. "What happens when one of them catches another one?" I asked.

"One gets eaten."

"Oh."

"Come take a look," he said. He shuffled down the aisle a little way and stopped at another aquarium. This one was full of fish, a dozen or more, of all different sizes and colors. Tesselman tapped on the glass, and they all flocked over to see what was doing. He shook a little fish food into the water, and the fish went nuts, trying to get at the stuff. One of them went out of his head completely, and started to swell up like a balloon. "That's a Beta," Tesselman told me. "Siamese fighting fish. They actually do fight them in Siam, like cockfighting in this country in the old days. I'm told it's a fine gambling sport. No likelihood of a fixed fight."

"Good-looking fish," I said, repeating the compliment. This Beta was good-looking at that. He looked like a new car, with all the pastel colors, and the fins, and all the rest of it.

"They're my beauties," said Tesselman. Then he looked up at me again. "You want to talk about poor Mavis."

"Yes, sir."

"A terrible thing," he said. He puttered away from me again, his head turning from side to side as he looked at his fish, and I tried to connect him with Mavis St. Paul or anyone like her, but I failed. Then I tried to picture this fuddy-duddy little man as a political power, and I failed there, too. There had to be more to this man than he was showing me.

I walked along after him. "The police are looking for a man named Billy-Billy Cantell," I said.

"I know. They say he's a dope addict. He came to burglarize the apartment, and killed poor Mavis when she discovered him." He tapped at another aquarium and poured some more fish food in among the cannibals. "They haven't caught him yet, so far as I know," he said.

"I'm probably the only one who has seen him since the murder," I said.

I had his attention at last. He looked at me through his spectacles, no longer blinking. "You've seen him? Talked to him?"

"Yes, sir."

He looked away from me, studied the darting fish for a minute, then put the box of fish food and the net down and said, "You aren't interested in tropical fish. Come to my study."

He led the way and I followed him, walking slowly, matching his old man's pace. We went down the horror-movie hall and into his study, a high-ceilinged room, dark and windowless, the walls covered with jammed bookcases. Tesselman switched on the indirect lighting, motioned for me to sit in the brown-leather chair facing the desk, and himself sat behind the desk, hands folded in his lap, looking at me with pursed-lip attention. He looked out of place behind that desk, smaller and more fragile than ever in back of all that broad, empty mahogany. The wood of the desk was dark and rich and highly polished, and looked as though it should be warm to the touch. A telephone and an ashtray were the only items on the desktop.

"Did he tell you about the killing?" Tesselman asked me.

"Not exactly. He didn't see it. He fell asleep in a doorway or an alley somewhere, earlier in the evening, and when he woke up he was in Miss St. Paul's apartment. She was lying on the floor, already dead. He was terrified and ran away, leaving his hat and fingerprints behind. He came directly to me, asking for help, but the police showed up and he ran away again. I haven't been able to locate him since."

"He doesn't remember murdering poor Mavis?"

"He doesn't think he did. And neither do I."

He frowned. "Why not?"

"Three reasons," I told him. I counted them off on my fingers. "First, Billy-Billy himself. He's a meek, nervous, quiet little guy whose only defense is running, and whose only offense is dope. He isn't the type who kills. When he gets in a jam, he folds up. Second, he doesn't carry a knife or any other weapon. He's afraid to. He knows it's nothing but a cheap conviction if the police pick him up and find a weapon on him, and he also knows he'd never be able to use a knife. Third, someone called the police right after the murder, and made the tip-off. That meant someone besides Billy-Billy and Miss St. Paul was present. The real killer."

Tesselman was studying me carefully, lips pursed out in concentration. The fussy little man was almost completely gone now, replaced by a shrewd and silent man who could be relied on to be nobody's fool.

He said, "The first two reasons you gave are meaningless. This Cantell isn't the killing type, and he doesn't carry a weapon. You are talking about his character and his logic. But you yourself said he was taking dope, that he had taken so much he lost consciousness. Rules of character and logic don't apply."

I shrugged. It was too early to start arguing over individual points. "There's only the phone call," I said.

"Possibly only a witness," he said.

"Possibly, but not very probably. Where was this witness? If he was in the apartment, why didn't he come to Miss St. Paul's assistance? Dope or no dope, Billy-Billy Cantell is a puny little weakling who'd have a tough time taking candy away from a baby. If he'd attacked Miss St. Paul with a knife, she could have taken the knife away from him, held him down, and called the police. He's no raging monster, believe me."

"We were talking about the witness," he said.

"The witness, yes. Where was he? In the apartment? If so, he was either the murderer or an accessory to the murder, because he didn't even try to stop it."

"He might have been in the building across the street, and saw the murder through the window."

"I haven't seen Miss St. Paul's apartment," I said. "I'll have to leave it to you whether that's possible or not."

He looked startled for a second, and then he frowned down at his folded hands, thinking. Finally, he said, "You're right. He couldn't have been across the street.

Mavis was killed in the living room, and she always kept the living-room drapes closed in the summer. Because of the air conditioning."

"Then he had to be in the apartment."

"Yes." He looked at me, frowning, and said, "I've only just met you. I have no way of knowing how trustworthy you are, and I didn't hear anything about a phone call before this. Would you be offended if I checked that story?"

"Not at all," I said. "May I smoke in the meantime?"

"Of course." He pushed the ashtray across the desk toward me, and picked up the phone. I lit a cigarette and smoked energetically while Tesselman talked rapidly to somebody he called "John." He said he would wait, and we avoided looking at one another until John came back and answered his question.

When he hung up, Tesselman looked at me and said, "All right. Where does it go from there?"

"Cantell passed out," I said, "earlier that evening, in a doorway or an alleyway or maybe even on the sidewalk. Our man murdered Miss St. Paul, left the apartment, picked up Cantell, brought him back to the apartment, left him there and phoned the police. If Cantell hadn't come to, and gotten out of there just before the police showed up, the case would have been closed by now, and Cantell would be on his way to the chair, while the guy who really did kill Miss St. Paul would get off scot-free."

"There's another possibility," he said. "Cantell murdered Mavis, left the apartment, spoke to someone else before he went to you, and that someone else immediately phoned the police."

"I'm afraid not, sir," I said. "The police arrived at the apartment before Billy-Billy had gone a block. He saw them. And I was the only person he talked to."

"On both of those counts, you have to take his word for it."

"Why not? At the time, there was no reason for him to be lying. If he'd been to somebody else, he would have told me. He wanted me to help him, he wouldn't have lied to me."

"All right, I'll grant that. Provisionally. I'm still bothered by one point."

"Sir?"

"This murderer of yours was taking a very grave risk when he returned to the apartment, carrying Cantell. If he had been seen, his whole plan would have fallen apart."

"That's a quiet block at that time of night. And I assume there's no doorman at Miss St. Paul's building, and that the elevator is self-service."

"Yes, you're right. Still, why did he go to so much trouble? Why didn't he just leave after the murder and let it go at that?"

"He must be somebody who has a pretty good motive for wanting Miss St. Paul dead. If the police didn't have another suspect handy, they might poke around until they found that motive."

"All right. Then, why Cantell?"

"It could have been anybody. Any bum he ran across,

sleeping one off so soundly he wouldn't wake up when he was moved."

"That also sounds unlikely. Cantell would certainly have remembered being moved."

"Not necessarily. Last night, I tried to wake a friend of his, to find out if he knew where Billy-Billy might be. The friend was doped up at the time. I moved him, slapped him, walked him around, put him in a tub of cold water, and it took me almost half an hour to wake him up to the point where he recognized me. And I was *trying* to wake him up. Our killer didn't want to wake Cantell, he just wanted to move him. That isn't difficult at all."

Tesselman leaned back in his chair and studied the titles of the books on the shelves nearest him. "It's plausible," he said at last. "It makes sense."

"It's the only way that does make sense," I said.

"All right. You have me three-quarters convinced. Now you want something from me, or you wouldn't be here. What is it?"

"I want two things," I said. "First, you put a bug in somebody's ear, somebody in the Police Department, about getting this case solved fast, putting the murderer behind bars right away."

"I may have mentioned I was interested in the case," he said. "But I certainly don't control the Police Department."

"I know that, sir. But the police are getting too eager. They're trying to force Ed Ganolese to turn Cantell over to them. They're disrupting operations right on down the line, with raids and arrests and all the rest of it. They're fouling the organization up just when I need it running smoothly, so I can put it to work looking for the guy who framed Billy-Billy."

"The Police Department is doing this?" He sounded honestly surprised.

"Yes, sir. And the worst part of it is that we don't have Billy-Billy. I'm the only one who's seen him, and he ran away from me when the cops showed up. Nobody knows where he is."

"And you want me to take the bug out of my somebody's ear, is that it?"

"Yes, sir."

"All right, I'll see what I can do. Now, what was the second thing you wanted from me?"

"Mavis St. Paul," I said. "The killer knew her, and had a reason for wanting her dead. I didn't know her, and I don't know anybody who knew her. I'd like you to fill me in, tell me who her friends were, who her enemies were, who might have wanted to kill her."

There was a change in his expression then, too slight and too subtle to define. But something of the fussy old gentleman who had been puttering around with his tropical fish was back in Tesselman's manner all at once, and he said, "I don't believe poor Mavis had any enemies. She was a lovely girl, a beautiful girl." He leaned forward, and his eyes, behind the spectacles, were blinking again. "A beautiful girl," he repeated. "She had a lovely singing voice, clear and soft. Not operatic, really, not strong enough for that, just a soft and lovely voice, like a bell. She had planned to return to her acting lessons, you know. She had a great deal of natural talent. A friend of mine is a backer of Broadway musical comedies, and I had already talked to him about her. As soon as she had had more training and more experience, he would have found a place for her. She had a wonderful future ahead of her. Such a beautiful girl."

"There was no one you knew of who disliked her?"

"Who could dislike her? Such a sweet girl. She was only a child. Everyone loved her."

"Who were her friends, then? The people who knew her?"

"I never knew many of them," he said. "Her old roommate could probably help you there, more than I. Her name is Betty Benson."

"Yes, I've already heard of her. I have her address, but I haven't been to see her yet."

"She's the one who could help you." His hands were atop the desk now, bony and fidgeting, and he sat staring at them. "Such a lovely girl," he said. "Everybody loved her."

Someone knocked at the door. Tesselman looked up, called out, "Come in," and the butler stuck his head around the door to say, "Mabel's giving birth, Mr. Tesselman."

"Oh!" Tesselman changed at once. Now he was completely the puttering old codger again, without the wistful overtones caused by the subject of Mavis St. Paul. He got to his feet and scurried around the huge desk. "Come along," he said to me. "This should be worth seeing!"

He hurried down the hall, running in the strained shuffle which is the old man's trot, and the butler and I followed him. The three of us clustered around the tank holding Mabel and her new brood. Tesselman went to work with the midget butterfly net, transferring the newborn fish from the aquarium to a large Mason jar half-full of water. Mabel darted back and forth, chasing her young, so infuriated at the net that kept getting in her way that she smacked straight into the glass side of the tank.

Tux said, "Beautiful, ain't they, Mr. Tesselman?"

"Beautiful," said Tesselman. His voice was the same as it had been when he was describing Mavis St. Paul.

I looked at this old man, and he just didn't ring true. The changes were too fast, there was something calculated about them. There was no difference between his extolling the late Mavis St. Paul and his praising the beauty of his cannibal tropical fish.

There wasn't anything else for me to do here, and Tesselman had apparently forgotten me and our conversation completely anyway, so I said, "Well, I guess we've covered it, Mr. Tesselman. I'll be getting on."

"Oh, yes," he said, distracted. He paused to blink at me. "You see Betty Benson," he said. "She'd be able to tell you about Mavis's friends." He went back to work with the net.

"I'll do that," I said. "Remember about the bug, will you?"

"I will, I'll call this afternoon. Got you, you little squirmer!"

"I can find the door," I said.

"Keep me informed," he said, but he didn't look away from the fish.

"Yes, sir, I will."

I went down the horror-movie hall and the *Gone with the Wind* staircase, by the *Life* contemporary living room, and outside to my Mercedes. I sat in the car for a while, trying to figure it out. Tesselman had showed me about three different faces, and the shrewd and calculating face was the only one that rang true. The business with the fish could be considered simply a relaxation of his shrewdness, the purpose of any hobby.

But why the crocodile tears over Mavis St. Paul? For some reason, he'd wanted me to think Mavis St. Paul had meant something special to him, something more than a casual mistress. Why? The answer to that one might prove interesting.

Chapter Nine

On the way back to town, I stopped at a roadside phone booth and called Ed, to tell him the good news about Tesselman. "The dogs," I told him, "have been called off." He told me there was still no word from or about Billy-Billy, and I asked him which he wanted me to work on especially, finding Billy-Billy or finding the cutie. "Never mind Billy-Billy," he said. "Wherever he's hiding out, it's good enough to keep the cops from finding him. Get the bastard who started all this, and we won't have to worry about Billy-Billy at all."

So my next stop was Betty Benson, who lived in the Village, on Grove Street near Sheridan Square.

Grove Street, naturally, was a one-way. The *other* way. I tried circling the block, which is virtually impossible in Greenwich Village, and after a while I wound up on Grove Street, parked between two Volkswagens, a block and a half from the address I wanted.

The building Betty Benson lived in was an old one, converted half a dozen times from whatever had been its original role in life. There was a buzzer-release system on the downstairs door. I rang the bell next to "Benson," and after a minute the buzzer sounded and I pushed the door open.

Betty Benson lived on the third floor, and it was a walk-up. I was puffing by the time I got to the third floor, and I remembered I'd only had a few hours' sleep since yesterday. I stopped at the head of the stairs, to get my wind and my bearings, and looked around. All the doors on this floor were closed, but I saw a peephole open in one of them, so I walked over and peeped back. There was an eye looking out at me. "Miss Benson?" I said.

Her voice was muffled by the door. "What do you want?"

The standard New York greeting. The less a New Yorker has, the more firmly convinced he is that everybody in the world is waiting, just outside his apartment, to take it all away from him.

"I'm a friend of Ernest Tesselman's," I said. It wasn't strictly accurate, but this looked like a good time for name-dropping, and if this was Mavis St. Paul's friend and former roommate, she should know who Ernest Tesselman was.

Apparently she did, and wasn't very happy about it, because she said, "Go away."

"I'd like to talk to you about Mavis," I said.

"I already talked to the police. Go away."

"This won't take long," I promised.

"Just go away," she insisted. "I don't want to talk to anybody."

"What are you so jumpy about?" I asked her.

"After what happened to Mavis?"

"Don't be silly. I'm a friend of Ernest Tesselman's, and I want to talk to you."

"I'm not going to let you in," she said.

"I'll wait out here," I told her. "You'll come out sooner or later."

"I'll call the police."

"Ask for Grimes," I said. "He's a friend of mine."

The peephole snapped shut, and I heard her moving around inside. I wondered if she really would call the cops. I wished I didn't have to have anything to do with this chick. Nervous females make me upset.

After a couple of minutes, the peephole opened again, and the eye came back. She said, "Why don't you go away?"

"I want to talk to you."

"Talk from out there."

"Sure," I said. "That's all right with me." I dug a pencil and notebook out of my inside jacket pocket. "I'd like to know the names of people who knew Mavis. Her friends and her enemies."

"Who are you?"

"I told you. A friend of Ernest Tesselman's."

"What do you want to know about Mavis for?"

"I'm looking for her killer."

"You mean the dope fiend?"

"No. He didn't do it."

"Then who?"

"I don't know yet."

"Why do you say the dope fiend didn't kill her?"

"Because I talked to the dope fiend, and he said he didn't, and everybody knows that dope fiends never lie."

"You *talked* to him?"

"That's right."

"Who *are* you?"

"I told you. A friend of Ernest Tesselman's."

"Why are you looking for the killer?"

"Mr. Tesselman asked me to." Another inaccuracy, but a lot easier and faster than the truth.

"What does he care?"

"He liked Mavis."

"Hah," she said. "Ernest Tesselman doesn't like anybody but himself. And his fishes," she added, as an afterthought.

"What makes you say that?"

"I just do."

"Do you suppose I could come inside?" I asked her. "You could make coffee, and we could sit down like civilized people and have a chat about dope fiends and fishes and Ernest Tesselman and Mavis St. Paul and all sorts of interesting things."

"Don't make fun," she said.

"I'm not making fun," I told her. "I'm very, very serious. I just climbed two long flights of stairs, and I didn't get much sleep last night, and I feel like sitting down."

She thought about it for a minute, then said, "Are you armed?"

"Of course not. What do you take me for?"

"Open your coat," she said.

So I opened my coat and showed her that I didn't have a shoulder holster. Then I turned around and raised my coat tails so she could see I didn't have a gun in my hip pocket. I faced her again and said, "Shall I hike up my pant-legs? Maybe I have a knife strapped to my leg."

"I have to be careful," she said. "After what happened to Mavis—"

"Certainly. An ounce of caution is worth a pound of plasma."

The peephole closed again, a chain rattled, and the door swung open. She studied me for a second, holding tight to the doorknob, testing to see whether or not I planned to leap at her, and then she stepped back and to the side. "Come on in, then," she said.

I went on in. The living room was long and narrow, painted gray, and was so completely Greenwich Village in style that it looked more like a stage setting than an actual living room. It was one trite, standard bit after another. The piece of gray driftwood on the black, vaguely Japanese coffee table. The modern painting, looking like a broken stained-glass window, centered on one of the long walls. A low bookcase constructed of one-by-twelve boards separated by unmortared bricks. A cheap record player on an obviously second-hand table, with five or six long-playing record albums lying beside it. Three empty Chianti bottles were tastefully suspended from the wall between the two windows, and the windows themselves were covered with red burlap drapes. A couple of Moselle bottles, festooned with candle drippings, sat around on odd tables, and a hook in the middle of the ceiling showed where the mobile had once been hung, when mobiles were in fashion.

Betty Benson didn't go with the apartment. She

suited her name much better than that. Except for the
lack of little white stars in her eyes, she looked like a
Jon Whitcomb illustration for the *Saturday Evening
Post*. She was one of those sweet, sincere, All-American-
Girl, Junior-Prom, brainless types, with fluffy brown
hair, a smooth and rather blank face, and a good though
not spectacular body. She was dressed in a gray sweat-
shirt and pink pedal-pushers and in five years she would
have traded the driftwood and the Chianti bottles for a
washer-dryer and a husband, out in some suburban
development.

I knew very little about this type of broad, because
my work doesn't normally bring me in contact with
them. I'd known some way back in my college days,
but they'd bored me then and they bored me now. I
didn't know how to talk to this one to get her into the
mood to answer questions.

She closed the door and turned to face me. "If you
try anything," she said, "I can scream. And I left the
door unlocked. And the man next door is home, because he works nights."

"Darn," I said. "Then I guess I can't rape-murder
you after all."

I'd forgotten that chicks like this have absolutely no
sense of humor. She stood there for a second, trying to
figure out what her reaction to that one was supposed
to be, and finally gave up on it. "You can sit down anywhere," she said.

"Thanks." I avoided the black basket chair and sat
on the studio couch.

"You wanted to talk about Mavis," she said.

"Uh huh. I'd also like some coffee, if you've got some handy. I wasn't kidding about being behind in my sleep."

"All right. How do you like your coffee?"

"Black," I said. "One sugar."

"It's instant," she said doubtfully.

"That's all right," I told her. "I love instant." I hate instant.

"So do I," she said. She smiled. We had found a common ground.

I sat on the zebra-striped studio couch and waited, while she clanked silverware in the kitchenette. A whistling teakettle whistled, more silverware clanked, and she came back, walking carefully, holding two full cups of coffee out at arm's length.

"Let me help," I said, getting to my feet. I rescued one of the coffees, and we both sat down, me back on the studio couch, she in the basket chair across the room.

"You're a friend of Ernest Tesselman's?" she asked me. It was good to see I'd gotten through to her on that point.

"That's right," I said.

"And he sent you to look for whoever killed Mavis?"

"Right again."

"That seems awfully strange," she said.

"Why? They were more or less living together, weren't they? I imagine she was important to him."

She shook her head as she stirred her coffee. "It just doesn't seem like him," she said. "That dirty old man."

"Why do you say that?"

"Because that's what he is. He came here once, before Mavis went to live with him, and Mavis was out shopping or somewhere. He tried to seduce me. There he was, going with Mavis, and he knew I was Mavis's best friend, and he tried to seduce me. And he was old enough to be my grandfather."

"He's old enough to be Mavis's grandfather, too," I said.

"Mavis thought he could help her in her career."

"Did you think so?"

"He *could* have," she said. "But I bet he wouldn't have. Mavis never learned. She kept going off and sleeping with men who promised her the moon, and they were all the same, all nothing but liars. But she never did learn. She was always sure that this was the time, this man was telling the truth."

"Ernest Tesselman wasn't the only one, then," I said. I had the notebook and pencil ready. "Do you know who any of the others were?"

"Well, of course," she said. "Mavis was my best friend. She always lived here, uh, between men."

"Cy Something-or-other was first, wasn't he?"

"Not really," she said. "Alan Petry was first, but he doesn't count."

"Alan Petry?" I copied the name down in the notebook. "Who was he," I asked, "and why doesn't he count?"

"Well, it's been years since they've even seen each other," she said. "And Alan didn't have any money or prospects or anything like that, so it was never anything really serious between them."

"You're making Mavis St. Paul sound like the original gold digger," I said.

"Well, she was," said Betty Benson. "I mean, she's dead now, and she was my best friend and all, but still and all the truth is the truth. Mavis was a very sweet person, a wonderful person to get along with, but she was awfully mercenary."

"So she was never serious about this"—I looked at the name I'd written—"this Alan Petry. Was he serious about her?"

"No, not really. At least, I don't think so. I never knew him very well. He was just another boy taking acting lessons. He wasn't too awfully talented, and I guess he realized it, because he dropped out of Paul's class shortly after I met him. He and Mavis just enjoyed living together, that was all. They had a good time together for a while, and then it was all over."

"Where is he now, do you have any idea?"

"I think he lives out on Long Island somewhere," she said. "At least, he did the last I heard. He's married and has a family now. He gave up acting completely and became a policeman."

"A cop?" I made a note after Petry's name.

"He gave up acting right after Mavis left him. He took the examination, whatever examination it is you have to take if you're going to be a policeman, and passed and got the job. Then he got married—I don't think I ever met the girl he married—and moved out on Long Island somewhere. I haven't seen him for years."

"Then Cy—what is Cy's last name?"

"Grildquist," she said.

"That's it, Grildquist. He came after Petry?"

"Well, no. Mavis went with Paul Devon for a while. The acting teacher."

"The one she and Petry were taking lessons from."

"That's right. I'm in his class, too. That's where I met Mavis. She and Paul never lived together, but they spent a lot of time together. You know. Mavis didn't have to pay anything for the classes."

"Sweet girl," I said.

"She was." Betty Benson bridled, as the saying goes. "Nobody is perfect, you know. Not you or me or anybody. Mavis was a *very* sweet girl, but she just happened to be mercenary, that's all."

"Okay. I'm not knocking her. Who comes after Paul Devon?"

"Cy Grildquist," she said.

"At last." I wrote the name down. "She lived with him, didn't she?"

"For about six months, and then she came back here. He promised her all kinds of things, but she finally realized he had no intention of making the promises good. So she left him."

"Hard feelings?"

"She had, for a little while. He didn't, though. He was ready for another girl by then, anyway."

"You sound as though you don't like Mr. Grildquist."

"I don't," she said. "He's a fat, sloppy old lecher, and you can't believe a word he says."

"Mavis had a habit of picking nice boyfriends, didn't she?"

"She wanted to be rich," said Betty Benson simply. "So she stayed with rich men."

"Okay, that makes sense. Who was next on the rich-man parade?"

"You make it sound a lot harsher than it was. Mavis wasn't a—a prostitute, or anything like that."

"I know. She was only mercenary."

"A lot of people are," she said.

"Granted. Who came after Grildquist?"

"A man named Ricardo. Johnny Ricardo. He owns a nightclub or something."

"Okay. How long did that one last?"

"Just a few months. Then she came back here to live again, until she met Charles Morgan."

I scribbled Morgan's name down, and said, "Who was he?"

"He had something to do with television, I don't know what. Then Ernest Tesselman was after that, and that's all."

"I see." I looked at the list of names. "Were any of these men married?" I asked her.

"I don't know," she said. Then she thought about it for a minute. "Cy Grildquist is married. Or he was then, but I think he's divorced now. That happened after Mavis broke up with him. Johnny Ricardo—I think he was divorced then, and now he's married again."

"What about Paul Devon?"

"No, he isn't married. He was once, when he was very young, but she died in an accident. He never married again. He was very much in love with her, and all broken up when she died. He had to go away to a sanitarium and everything."

"When did all this happen?"

"Oh, years ago."

"How do you know about it?"

"Oh, everybody knows about it. Everybody in his classes, I mean. Whenever he hears her name, his eyes get all misty."

"I see. What about Charles Morgan? Is he married? Or was he, at the time?"

"I don't know," she said. "I don't remember. I'm sure Mavis must have told me—Mavis told me about everything—but I don't remember whether he was married or not. Not that it makes any difference any more."

"Why not?"

"Well, he's dead. He died about a year ago. Mavis thought he was going to leave her a whole lot of money in his will. He told her he would, but he didn't. I forget who got his money. There wasn't much of it, anyway. Not as much as Mavis thought there would be."

I wrote "Dead a year ago" after Charles Morgan's name on my list, and said, "Is there anybody you know of who might hate Mavis, or might have wanted to kill her?"

"Of course not." She looked at me as though she thought I was crazy for even suggesting such a thing. "Nobody could ever hate Mavis," she said. "Oh, she was awfully trying at times, of course. Everybody is, in one way or another. Mavis was awfully lazy and wanted to be waited on all the time. She'd never take her turn to do the dishes and things like that. But she was an awfully sweet person. She was never catty or anything, never talked about anybody behind their back or anything like that. She was a good friend. Everybody liked Mavis."

"Had you seen much of her lately?"

"Oh, sure. She'd come over and chat all the time."

"Was she worried about anything? Did she act as though she were afraid or upset about anything at all?"

"Not at all. She was in seventh heaven. She thought Ernest Tesselman was going to get her a big part in some musical comedy or something. She even thought he was going to marry her. She was going to go talk to a lawyer about a divorce and everything."

"A divorce?"

"Well, certainly. She couldn't get married again without getting a divorce first."

"I didn't know she'd been married."

"Oh, it was years and years ago. She was married in her home town, before she came to New York. There's an air base or something out there, and she married somebody from the base. She was a legal secretary or something at the base, and that's how she met him. Then he deserted her, after they'd only been married a little while, and she came to New York. That's why she was so mercenary about men. She'd married for love once, and all she'd gotten was heartache."

"What was her married name, do you know?"

"I don't think she ever told me. It wasn't St. Paul, I know that. That was just a stage name. She named herself after Paul Devon, because he was her acting teacher. But she never told me what her husband's name was. She didn't like to talk about that part of her life. It was awfully painful for her."

"I imagine so." I looked at the list of names, and read them aloud. " 'Alan Petry, Paul Devon, Cy Grildquist, Johnny Ricardo, Charles Morgan, Ernest Tesselman.' Was there anybody else particularly close to her, that you know of?"

"No, that's all I know of," she said. "She would have told me, if there was anybody else. We told each other everything."

"How about women? Did she have many woman friends?"

"Only me. She didn't like most girls. She thought they were silly."

"I see." I tried to think of something else to ask her, but there wasn't anything. I got to my feet. "Thank you very much, Miss Benson," I said. "You've been a great help."

She stood up and walked to the door with me. "I think you ought to watch Ernest Tesselman," she said, "If he told you he was in love with Mavis, or anything like that, he was lying. He was just stringing her along, like all the rest of them. He had no intention of marrying her, just as he had no intention of getting her into musical comedy."

"What makes you say that?"

"Mavis was tone deaf. She couldn't carry a tune."

Chapter Ten

Back in the Mercedes, I spent a useless couple of minutes staring at my list of names and trying to figure out what to do next. I should go talk to these people, find out about them, narrow the list of suspects down to the one name that would spell cutie, but I just couldn't concentrate on the problem. It had been relatively cool in Betty Benson's apartment, but outside it was as hot and muggy as ever. It was four o'clock in the afternoon and I'd had about two hours sleep in the last thirty, and I was too groggy to think. The world was just going to have to wait for a few hours, while I got caught up on my rest.

That was the only decision I was capable of making right then. It was time to go to sleep. I started the Mercedes, and drove down toward Sheridan Square, and fiddled around among the one-way streets until I finally managed to head myself uptown. At one point, I thought I saw a car I kind of recognized and I waved, and then I forgot it.

I drove home, left the Mercedes with the day kid at the garage, and slogged through the humidity to my building. The air conditioning inside was nice, but no longer enough to revive me. I leaned against the wall of the elevator all the way up to my floor.

Ella was in the living room, bright and chipper, when

I walked in. She was dressed in a white peasant blouse and a full white skirt with Aztec designs on it in gold, and she looked so goddam cool and alert I could have kicked her teeth in out of pure envy. I stood in the middle of the living room and peeled my suitcoat off.

"Poor Clay," she said, taking the suitcoat from me. "You look tired."

"I am tired," I told her. "I want to take a vacation. I want to go away somewhere. Maybe Alaska." I ripped off my tie, handed it to her, and went to work on the buttons of my shirt.

"You should take a shower," she said. "And then go to bed for a while."

"You're absolutely right," I said. I let her lead me through the apartment to the bedroom, and between us we got my clothes off. Then she took me into the bathroom, stood me in the shower, and turned the water on. It was cold at first, and I shivered a bit, but then it warmed up and felt fine. I stood there for a long while, not thinking at all, just enjoying the feel of the lukewarm water on my skin, and then I stepped out onto the mat and Ella toweled me dry. She brought me back to the bedroom, helped me into bed, and tucked the nice crisp sheets in around me. She kissed me on the forehead, playing the Little Mother role to the hilt, and said, "Have a good sleep."

I murmured something, closing my eyes, and the goddam doorbell sounded off.

"Oh, no," said Ella.

"I'm not home," I said. "I've gone away."

"All right," she said. She left the bedroom, and I closed my eyes again.

I was just drifting off to sleep when she came back. She touched my shoulder. "Clay, it's the police," she said. "They want to talk to you."

I opened my eyes, and saw Grimes standing in the doorway. "Up and at 'em, Sleeping Beauty," he said. "We're going for a little ride."

"You want to sublet this goddam place?" I asked him.

"Get up and get dressed," he said. "Snap it up."

I stared at him, wondering what the hell had happened to Tesselman. Hadn't he come through on his promise to calm the cops? Or was that lousy fish of his still giving out with babies? "What's wrong now?" I asked him.

"Move," he said. "Unless you want to be booked in the buff."

"Booked? Booked for what?"

"You got it wrong, Clay," he said. "*I* ask the questions. All you do is get up and get dressed." He turned to Ella. "If you wouldn't mind—" he started.

"It's all right," I said. "She's seen me in the raw."

"Nevertheless," he said.

"I'll be in the living room," she said, and went away.

I pushed the sheet to one side and got out of bed. As I padded around the room, gathering clothes, I tried to figure it out. Tesselman should have given the all-clear signal a couple of hours ago. Unless the son of a bitch had double-crossed me. But why should he? He didn't have any percentage in letting Mavis St. Paul's killer get away.

Unless Ernest Tesselman was the killer himself. I sat on the edge of the bed, in the middle of putting on my socks, and let that little thought play around inside my head. Did it make sense? Tesselman kills her, drags in Billy-Billy to play stand-in, and uses his influence to see to it that the cops don't look any further than the patsy. Did it make sense?

"Come on, Clay," said Grimes. "Quit stalling."

I didn't want to go to jail, I really didn't want to go to jail. This was a notion that hadn't occurred to me before, and I needed time to think it out, time to poke around and see if it made sense. Tesselman tried to give me the impression he felt strongly about Mavis St. Paul, he'd been going to help her land a job in a musical comedy. He'd told her he planned to marry her. But he just hadn't rung true with his eulogy for Mavis, and Betty Benson had supported the idea that Tesselman was faking his feelings for the girl. Maybe they'd had a fight. It could have happened, Mavis could have found out he was just stringing her along. They argued, he lost his temper, stabbed her—

"You want to go with no shoes on?" Grimes asked me.

"Listen, Grimes," I said. "I don't want to go at all. What is this? You guys still playing dragnet for Billy-Billy Cantell? I told you I don't know where he is, and I still don't know where he is, and if I knew where he was I'd deliver him to Centre Street personally."

"Talk at the station," he said. "You'll get all the chance you want."

You can't argue with cops, you can't reason with them. They get an idea into their heads and that's it. If an atom bomb were to go off right outside the window at that point, they would still take me right through the fallout to the station.

I knew better than to try to talk to a cop. I'd play their game, get out as soon as I could, and get back to work. I finished dressing and walked through the apartment to the living room, Grimes right behind me.

Ella was in the living room, sitting in the chair next to the phone, and the other two cops who went everywhere with Grimes lately were both standing by the door.

Ella looked over at me and said, "They won't let me call Clancy."

"They have no respect for due process of the law," I told her. "Call him as soon as we leave."

"All right," she said. "It isn't anything serious, is it, Clay?"

I didn't know whether it was or not. "No," I said. "It isn't serious. These guys just can't think of anything else to do, since they lost their pinochle deck."

"Come on," said Grimes.

"I'll call him right away," Ella promised, as we left.

We went down the hall to the elevator, and Grimes said, "She doesn't deserve you. She seems like a pleasant girl."

"She is," I said. "Listen, is this trip really necessary?"

"Yes."

The elevator door opened, and the four of us stepped inside, which crowded things a bit. "I really don't know where Billy-Billy is," I said. "You can hold me forever, and I still won't know."

"This has nothing to do with Cantell," he said.

The elevator started down then, but that wasn't what gave me the butterfly feeling in my stomach. "It isn't Cantell?"

"You know damn well it isn't," he said.

"How do I know all this?"

"Because you got to somebody," he told me. "I don't know who it was you got to, but we heard the word. Ease off on the Cantell search. Don't make life so difficult for the syndicate." He twisted his mouth in a grimace of disgust. "Sometimes," he said, "I wish I was President. Just for one day, just for twenty-four hours."

"So you're going to give me a hard time for something else, is that it? Sour grapes, is that it?"

"We'll talk at the station," he said.

"You're hell on wheels, Mr. Grimes," I said, but I wasn't really interested in the conversation any more. Tesselman had come through after all. He'd called off the cops, to give me a better chance to find out who had killed his girlfriend and framed Billy-Billy. So where did that put the Tesselman-as-killer theory? Right in the trash can.

And if Grimes wasn't after me for Cantell, what the hell was this? There was no sense asking him, he'd decided to play cute and close-mouthed, and he wouldn't tell me what day it was. Whatever it was, I hoped to hell it was something that Clancy could get me out of fast. I wasn't up to this kind of thing at the moment.

It was a long silent drive to the precinct station, and

it wasn't the precinct I'd thought we were going to. Which meant they didn't want Clancy to spring me right away. There were no formalities at the desk. We walked right by it, headed into the green-walled bowels of the building. So I wasn't even going to be booked yet. I could wait and guess and sweat it out until they finally decided to tell me what I was here for.

We all walked into a bare little room, and I knew I'd been through this game before. There were the chairs, one of them in the middle of the room and the rest scattered around against the walls. The lighting, I noticed, was normal, with no particular bright beam aimed at the chair in the center. As a matter of fact, there was enough outside light coming through the filthy windows so they didn't have to turn on the electric lights at all. Ashtray stands were dotted around the room, but none of them was near the center chair, which meant I wasn't going to be able to smoke. There was a water cooler in one corner of the room, and I knew that was something else I wouldn't be getting any of. Oh, this was going to be fun.

I didn't wait for anybody to give me directions. I just sat down in the chair in the middle of the room, and waited. Grimes and the other two cops drifted around the room for a couple of minutes, taking off their suit-coats and loosening their ties and shoving the chairs back and forth with grating noises. Grimes got himself a cup of water from the water cooler, which was behind me, and I heard it go *gurgle-gurgle*.

They finally decided to get started. Grimes led off, standing in front of me while the other two cops sat around in the background. "Where've you been all day?" he asked me.

"Here and there," I said.

"Names and addresses," he said.

"They slip my mind," I told him. "I want to make it clear that I'm not refusing to answer. It's just that I forget."

"You forget where you've been all day?"

"Yes, sir, I do. I forget where I've been all day. It was awful hot outside, that probably explains it. I do remember one thing. I didn't go anywhere with air conditioning."

One of the other cops spoke up. "How long you been shacking with the broad in your apartment?" he asked me.

That one surprised me. "A few weeks," I said.

"You figuring to drop her?"

"No." What the hell was he leading up to?

Grimes took over again. "Who was living with you before her?" he asked.

"Why?"

"I asked first," he said.

I was confused as hell, and it took me a minute to think of the broad's name. She was one of those big-breasted blondes, she looked like a million dollars and she was worth maybe fifteen cents in the rack. What the hell was her name? Then I thought of it. "Anita Merriwell," I said. "A dancer at La Copla."

"Before her?"

"How the hell do I know? Do you think I keep a

goddam record?" This line of questioning didn't make any sense at all. It didn't seem to be going anywhere. I couldn't figure out what the hell was going on, and when I can't figure out what's going on I get nervous. Unconsciously, I reached into my pocket for my cigarettes. I no sooner got them out than Grimes reached out and took the pack away from me. "Mind if I have a cigarette?" he asked me.

"Yes."

"I know you're kidding," he said. He took a cigarette out of the pack, then took three more. "For later," he explained. "You don't mind, do you?"

"Yes," I said.

One of the other cops came over. "I'd like to bum a smoke, too," he said.

"Sure," said Grimes. "Clay doesn't mind." He handed him the pack, and the guy took four and then carried it over to cop number three, who also took four cigarettes and then crumpled the pack and threw it into a corner.

Grimes grinned at me. "Sorry, Clay," he said. "I guess they're all gone. None left for you."

"That's okay," I told him. "I've been trying to give them up for weeks."

He lit one of my cigarettes and blew smoke in my face. The other two were also smoking, and none of them seemed to be inhaling. The room was a small one, and the windows were closed. It wouldn't take long for the place to fill up with smoke.

"Let's go back," said Grimes. "You were telling me who you went with before Anita Merriwell."

"I forget," I said. "I forget them all, every goddam one of them."

"That's a pity," said Grimes. "All those golden memories, all gone."

"Yeah," I said. "It's sure rough."

"Okay," said Grimes. "Then let's work our way forward. Who do you figure will be next? After—what did you say that girl's name was?"

"Anita Merriwell."

"No, no. I mean the new one."

"I didn't say."

"Well, say now."

"Ella."

"Ella what?"

"Ella Cinders."

"You're cute," said one of the other cops.

"I do my part," I told him.

"Anyway," said Grimes. "Who do you think will be next? After Ella?"

"I don't know," I said. "I haven't thought about it yet."

"What about Betty?" he asked me. "Is she next? Or is she one of the old ones?"

I just sat there and looked at him. Betty? Who the hell was Betty? "I don't know any Betty," I said.

"Sure you do."

I tried to think. Betty—Betty Benson? Mavis St. Paul's old roommate? He couldn't mean her, there wasn't anything there that would interest a cop, and if I asked him about her we'd go off onto another line of questioning, one I wouldn't particularly like.

Unless Betty Benson had called the cops on me, for some reason. Got suspicious after I left, called the cops, described me, told them I'd mentioned Grimes. It was a possibility, and not a very pleasant one. "What's this Betty's last name?" I asked.

"How many Bettys do you know?"

"None."

"Come on, Clay," said one of the other cops. "Quit playing around. We know you went to see her today. You left fingerprints all over the place. The coffee cup you used, everything."

So it *was* Betty Benson. "I thought you said this didn't have anything to do with Billy-Billy Cantell," I said.

Now it was their turn to look surprised, and I knew I'd opened my mouth once too often. If I hadn't been so damn tired, it never would have happened. They hadn't made the connection before, and now the surprise on their faces was changing to pleasure. They thought they had me, and I still didn't know what they thought they had me on.

One of the other cops snapped his fingers. "Betty Benson!" he said. "That was the St. Paul woman's old roommate!"

"Well, well," said Grimes. He looked at me and smiled. "So you wouldn't cover for Billy-Billy Cantell, is that right? You don't know where he is, is that right? If you see him, you'll turn him over to the law, is that right?"

"She knew something," said one of the other cops. He was getting excited. "She knew something, maybe saw Cantell, and he went to buy her off." He looked at me. "Isn't that right? She could make things rough for Cantell, so you went to pay her to keep her mouth shut, didn't you?"

"You're sick in the head," I told him. "How could things be rougher for him than they already are? You don't need anything more than you've got. You could convict him six times over without getting any more evidence than you have right now."

"So what were you doing there?" Grimes asked me.

"I forget," I said. I spent a second wondering when Clancy would get on the stick and spring me out of here. And then I took a second to wonder when Clancy would find me. Grimes wanted to hang something on me, but he must figure he wasn't ready yet, he didn't know enough yet, and he'd keep me in here, out of Clancy's grip, until he did know enough. And since I was a hell of a lot cleaner than I usually am, that meant I just might be in there forever.

"Come on, Clay," said Grimes. "You'll tell us about it sooner or later. Why not make it easier on all of us, and tell us sooner?"

"I still don't know what you want me to talk about," I said. "I still don't know what you dragged me in here for."

"Why not just tell us about Betty Benson? Maybe the reason will suddenly occur to you."

One of the other cops went behind me and got himself a drink of water. The water cooler went *gurgle-gurgle* again, and I thought about the fact that this room was small and hot and filling up with used cigarette smoke, and there wasn't any air conditioning. I licked my lips. I was thirsty already. Why the hell couldn't this have all happened in December instead of in August?

"Well, Clay?" said Grimes.

"Well what?"

"You went to see Betty Benson today, didn't you?"

"Apparently she already told you I did," I said. "So what?"

"What did you go there for?"

"I forget."

"What time did you get there?"

"I don't know. Somewhere around three-thirty."

"And when did you leave?"

"Around four sometime."

"So you were there for half an hour, is that right?"

"Something like that. Twenty minutes, half an hour."

"You left at four o'clock, is that right?"

"Around there somewhere."

"Okay," he said. "That'll do instead of a confession. Unless you'd like to give us a confession, too? We don't really need it, but it would make things a lot simpler."

"A confession to what? What the hell am I supposed to have done?" I was thinking back, trying to figure out what had happened. Betty Benson had threatened to call the police when I first showed up, but she'd seemed all right after that. And this didn't seem to be any simple complaint of the he-forced-his-way-into-my-apartment variety.

"Let's go sign you in," said Grimes. "You're going to be staying here for a while."

"Listen, do you mind telling me just what the hell this is all about? What's the goddam charge?"

"You can read over my shoulder," he said. "Come along, little man. Your roaming days are through."

So we walked back out to the desk, the four of us, where I was booked on suspicion of murder. The victim, Betty Benson. Time of death, approximately four o'clock this afternoon. And while I was still thinking that one over, I was led away to a little cell of my very own.

Chapter Eleven

You'd expect a jail in the largest and most modern city in the world to be something just a little bit special. You know, chrome-plated bars and Hollywood beds and color TV in every cell and guards wearing space helmets. But I'm sorry to say I have to report that the New York City clink has not kept stride with civic pride. The bars are the same old things, heavy and black and rough on the hands, and everything else is made of metal plates, like the hull of a battleship, painted bright yellow. Metal floor, metal ceiling, metal walls, metal slab suspended from chains, this last some city administration joker's idea of a bed. And everything clangs. They open a door way down at the other end of the corridor, and the clang runs through all the metal, sounding like somebody just hit a J. Arthur Rank gong right next to your ear.

Oh, it's a lovely place.

And I spent nineteen hours in it. I was booked at six P.M., and the little blue men took me away to my own private cell, with no Hollywood bed and no TV. But there was plumbing, over in the corner next to the metal slab bed, and my first task as a ward of the city was to clean this plumbing, which needed it in a bad way. That isn't my idea of a wild evening, believe me.

I signed in too late for supper (jugs are on the American Plan, meals included), so I didn't get fed anything until the next morning. And I didn't have a cellmate, of course. Most municipal clinks are one-man-cell operations, with a communal drunk tank off on another floor. Nor could I see any of my fellow boarders, since the cell across the corridor from me, the only one I could see into, was empty at the moment.

But there was a guy in the cell to my left, and we talked for a while, about this and that. He was old and stubbly, to judge from his wheezy voice, and we didn't have a hell of a lot to talk about, since we both carefully avoided mention of what we were in for. So after a while we played checkers. The way you play checkers in the jug, when you can't see your opponent, is simple. You take a piece of paper and mark out a checkerboard on it. The other guy does the same thing. Then you take twelve book matches and rip them in half. The halves with the head are your checkers and the other halves are the other guy's checkers. You number all the squares on the board, starting with the top left and working across each row, and then you call out the moves to each other, from number such-and-such to number so-and-so.

This old boy must have spent his whole life in one-man-cells, because he played this blind checkers like a champion, and I only beat him once in the two hours we played. Of course, part of that was the fact that I was too tired to see by then. I should have gone to sleep right away, since this was the first time in a hell of a while that I'd had some time to myself, but I kept expecting Clancy to ride to the rescue, and I wasn't looking forward to stretching out on that metal slab bed. But by eight o'clock, I just couldn't keep my eyes open any more, so I said good night to the guy next door, and went beddy-bye.

Did you ever try to sleep on a metal slab covered with a thin Army blanket? For a man who's used to the better things in life, like foam-rubber pillows and thick mattresses and female companionship in the rack, it's one hell of a come-down. Not that I had any trouble sleeping. I was out the second I lay down.

Actually, I never expected to be asleep for very long. I assumed Clancy would be along to spring me any minute. It shouldn't have been so very difficult to do. Clancy is an old pro at taking people out of jails, and I had now been booked all nice and legal, so there wasn't any problem about his finding me. Under normal circumstances, I should have been out by ten o'clock at the latest.

So I went to sleep at eight, expecting to sleep for two hours at the most, and the next thing I knew it was six-thirty in the morning, and I was awake.

And *how* I was awake. They've got a great little system for waking the boarders up in jail. At six-thirty A.M., they simultaneously clang every door they can find. The resulting racket can be heard for miles. I came up off that metal mattress of mine like an acrobat off a trampoline. That is one hell of a way to wake up, and is enough to make anybody antisocial forever. No wonder so many cons are repeaters. That morning clang, the first time they'd been jailed, made them malcontents for life.

I stood shaking in the middle of the cell for a minute or two, trying to orient myself. All the yellow lights went on, and all the yellow metal walls and ceiling were bright and painful, and reverberations of that clang were still going through my head.

Six-thirty in the goddam morning, and I was still here. My ears were trembling, my eyes were blinking, my hands were shaking, and my stomach was practicing judo holds with my liver. Besides that, my back hurt, my head ached, and my mouth had been filled with green mold from last week's bread.

And, to top it all off, a guard who'll get his in the afterlife brought me something he claimed was breakfast. It came in a metal tray, and the tray was cold. Things in metal trays are always the same temperature as the tray. The things in this tray were three soggy pancakes floating in some watered imitation maple syrup, and a scrawny apple. An apple!

It's an indication of how low I'd fallen in only twelve and a half hours that I ate the whole trayful, including the apple. Then I sat down on the plumbing to listen to my stomach bitch at me for a while, and I cursed Clancy Marshall up, down, and sideways.

The geezer next door wanted to play some more checkers, but I wasn't in the mood. I spent the morning thinking nasty thoughts.

I won't tell you what lunch was like. But I will tell you I ate every bite of it, every scurvy bite of it. And then I thought some more nasty thoughts.

When the guard came at one o'clock and unlocked my cell door (clang!), I had to restrain myself from hugging the bastard. I walked down that shiny yellow corridor in that people-zoo, and through a couple of doors, and I was a more or less free man, with my wallet back and everything.

Clancy was waiting for me out by the desk, but I wasn't ready to talk to Clancy yet. Clancy or anybody else.

"Ed wants to see you, keed," he said, smiling that hit-me smile of his.

"Ed can wait," I snarled at him. "Just like I did."

"They didn't want to let you go, boy," said Clancy. He managed to look aggrieved and to keep smiling at the same time. "It took some hard work to get you out, Clay."

"I am going home," I told him. "You can tell Ed that. You can tell him that I'm going home. And when I get there I am going to eat some real food and then I am going to go to sleep in a real bed and I am going to take a shower with real soap and real water, and when I am damn good and ready to see people I will let Ed know."

"Ed is kind of upset, Clay. Take the advice of a friend, don't make him mad at you."

"Why not? I'm mad at him. And at you, too. And everybody else. Tell Ed I'll see him when I get back to the human race."

I left him and took a cab home, and undertipped the driver for the hell of it. When he growled at me, I growled back. Then I growled at the doorman for good measure. I went up in the elevator, growling for practice, and found Ella waiting for me in the living room.

She came running across the room to me when I walked in. "Clay! They let you go!"

"I broke out," I told her. "I chewed through the bars."

"Clay," she said, "I was terrified for you. And when I read in the paper—"

"The paper! It got into the goddam paper?"

"All about the girl who was killed—"

"That's sweet," I said. "That's goddam sweet." I stomped around the room, kicking every piece of furniture I saw. It hadn't even occurred to me that I was going to show up in the newspapers, and now that it did occur to me it made me madder than ever. The cutie, the boy I was looking for, the boy who had started this whole thing in the first place by setting Billy-Billy up to fry for his murder—he was going to read the newspaper story about me, and he was going to see the connection between me and Billy-Billy, through the organization, and he was going to figure it out that I was after him. He was going to be on guard now, he wasn't going to feel safe any more. So he'd start covering himself on all sides. And if the job of finding him had been tough up to now, it was going to get even tougher from here on out.

I was sick of the whole thing. I was hot and tired and hungry and my bones ached and I didn't care if the whole world blew up. I might even stand by and cheer if it did. The hell with everything.

And then Ella said, "Clay, did you kill her?"

I stopped my pacing and stared at her. She was looking at me, serious and worried and very earnest, and I realized she thought maybe I did kill Betty Benson. And that put the capper on the whole thing.

"No," I said. "I did not kill the little bitch. I talked to her, and she told me all about Mavis St. Paul's string of rich boyfriends, and then I went away, and somebody else came along and killed her. The same guy who killed Mavis. Because Betty Benson was Mavis St. Paul's best friend."

"I'm glad you didn't, Clay," she said.

"That's damn nice of you," I said. "You're glad I didn't kill Betty Benson. That's peachy keen of you. I'm glad I meet with your goddam approval."

"Clay—"

"Well, let me tell you something," I said. "I didn't kill Betty Benson, but if Ed had told me to kill her, I would have. If Ed told me to kill you, I'd do it. I've killed people in the past, and I'll undoubtedly kill lots more people in the future, and if you don't like it nobody's keeping you here. And I'll tell you right now one guy I'm going to kill, and that's definite. The guy who started this whole mess, the one who killed Mavis St. Paul and Betty Benson. I am going to shoot that bastard down, and I am going to be *very* emotional about it. Do you hear me?"

"Clay, you're tired," she said.

"So what? You've been pussyfooting around the edges of my job, afraid to look in and see exactly what it is I'm doing. Well, *look* in. I'm Ed Ganolese's hired boy, goddam it to hell, and I do what he tells me and that means *anything* he tells me. And the fact that I'm in love with you doesn't change a goddam thing."

I stopped then, and stared at her. That last sentence had come out before I realized it. I hadn't known I was going to say that, I hadn't even known I was thinking it. Now, I just listened to the words, echoing in the room, and I couldn't say anything else.

"You're tired, Clay," she said. "You'd better get some sleep. Come on. Come on, Clay."

"All right," I said.

We went to the bedroom, and I undressed and went to bed, and the bed was incredibly soft after that miserable metal slab at the jail. I lay there listening to the echo of what I'd said to Ella, and I wondered at it.

Ella crawled into bed with me, and snuggled close against me. "I'll keep you warm," she said.

"Ella," I said.

"You're tired," she told me.

"Not that tired."

And after a while, I fell asleep, and I didn't hate the world so much any more.

Chapter Twelve

It was dark when I woke up, and Ella was gone. The clock said it was almost eight-thirty, so Ella was at work. She was a dancer, in the chorus at the Tambarin, and worked from eight till two.

I lay there in the pleasant darkness for a minute, not thinking about much of anything, and then my stomach let me know it was empty. I was starving, now that I thought about it, so I got out of bed, pulled on some clothes, stopped off at the bathroom to throw cold water on my face, and padded into the kitchen.

There was a note for me on the kitchen table: "Clay, There's a casserole in the oven. Turn the oven on to 350 for twenty minutes. Beer in the refrigerator. I love you. Ella."

I started the oven, had a couple of cups of coffee while waiting for the casserole to get ready, then ate and had a bottle of beer. And then I was ready to think.

I sat in my thinking chair in the living room, a bottle of beer in one hand and a cigarette in the other, and I looked around for a starting place. Betty Benson was as good a place to start as any. The same guy who had killed Mavis St. Paul had also killed Betty Benson. I didn't know why he'd killed Mavis, but I had a pretty good idea why he'd had to kill Betty Benson. She knew something that would link him to Mavis's killing. Whatever that knowledge was, she obviously hadn't realized its significance.

And the killer hadn't realized that I'd already talked to Betty Benson, before he got to her. Which meant there was a good chance that whatever it was he was trying to silence when he killed Betty Benson was in my notebook right now.

I went back out to the bedroom, found my notebook, and carried it back to my thinking chair and my beer. I studied the list of names Betty Benson had given me, and I felt very glum. I had a list of suspects a mile long.

There was Cy Grildquist, the producer Mavis had played around with. And Grildquist's wife was a possibility too, come to think of it. She'd been married to Grildquist, Mavis had shown up and departed, and now she wasn't married to him any more. There might be something doing there.

So there were two possibles. Johnny Ricardo, the nightclub owner, was a third. And Alan Petry, the ex-boyfriend turned cop. And Petry was married now, so that might bring in another suspect, Petry's wife. Next, Paul Devon, the drama teacher. And the husband out of Mavis's past, the guy she'd married in Belleville, Illinois. And Ernest Tesselman was still a good strong possibility. I wasn't about to give him a clean bill of health just yet.

Which made a grand total of eight people, out of whom I had met and talked to only one so far. Ernest Tesselman. The rest were strangers to me.

Well, they wouldn't be strangers long. I was about to go visiting. And, come to think of it, I had a whole goddam organization to help me. So far, they hadn't been any help at all, but that was about to change.

The nice thing about the organization I had behind me was that it had connections here, there and everywhere. There is hardly anybody living or working in New York who doesn't touch some part of the organization somewhere, either in his work or in his play. Put the right parts to work, and I could get information on almost anybody in town.

My first call was to Archie Freihofer. The names on my list were mostly men, rich men who liked expensive tail. Archie, being overseer of the *joie de vivre* girls, was the obvious guy to know these people.

"I read about you in the papers, baby," Archie cooed, when I told him who I was. "You got a good press agent."

"And you got a lousy sense of humor," I told him. "Listen, I've got some more checking for you to do."

"Anything, sweetie."

I gave him the names of Cy Grildquist, Johnny Ricardo, Paul Devon and, for the hell of it, Alan Petry. "All of these people knew Mavis St. Paul," I said. "I want to know when they saw Mavis last, what was the situation between them and Mavis lately, and where were they when Mavis was getting hers."

"I don't know, baby," he said. "The only one I know for sure is Johnny Ricardo. I can check him easy. The rest are strangers."

"Maybe some of the girls know them."

"I'll ask around."

"Good boy."

Next, I called Fred Maine, my bought cop. "There's a cop somewhere in New York," I told him, "name of Alan Petry. I'd like you to get me some information on him."

"Sure thing, Clay," he said. "What's up?"

"I'm not exactly sure," I said. You do not give bought cops extraneous information. "I just follow orders."

"What do you want to know, Clay?"

"Where was he all afternoon yesterday," I said. "And I hear he's married. I'd like to know what his home life is like, is he content to be married or does he play around? And if he plays around, does Mrs. Petry know it?"

"Gee, Clay," he said doubtfully. "I don't know. Stuff like that might be tough to find out."

"See what you can do," I said, and he promised he would.

Next, Paul Devon, the drama teacher. How to put the organization to work on him? I thought about it for a minute, and there was my connection. Drama teachers teach young actors and actresses. Young actors and actresses are part of the arty Greenwich Village world, and are prime customers for the cheaper drugs, particularly marijuana. So I called Junky Stein, who's The Man for that area, distributor to all the retailers downtown.

He was home, which was lucky, and when I told him I wanted some information, he said, "Name it."

"I'm interested in a guy named Paul Devon," I said. "Drama teacher over in the Village. I want to know any and all connections between him and a girl named Mavis St. Paul."

"*That* broad! Because of her, I spent four hours in a goddam jail cell."

"Don't feel bad, I spent nineteen."

"I heard about that, Clay. That was a rough deal."

"Yeah, well, that's the way it goes. I also want to know where Paul Devon was yesterday afternoon, especially around four o'clock."

"I'll see what I can get, Clay," he said.

Cy Grildquist was next. I thought about him for a while. Cy Grildquist, he produces plays on Broadway. Therefore, he works with about a million unions, the stagehands' union and the actors' union and the electricians' union and the designers' union and the ushers' union and the theater-managers' union and half a dozen other unions. And one of the pies in which Ed Ganolese has a finger is the New York City union movement. There is a fantastic amount of money in a union, and Ed wouldn't pass up a thing like that for anybody.

So I called a union man named Bull Rocco, a boy who is strong on the rights of labor, particularly on the rights of labor to unionize and to pay dues. "Bull," I said. "This is Clay. I wonder if you could do a little checking for me."

"I read about you in the papers, Clay," he said. Despite his name, Bull Rocco is a New Look union boy, complete with tie and clean shirt. "That was a pity."

"It sure was," I said. "You know anybody named Cy Grildquist?"

"Sure," he said. "He's got a play on Broadway right

now. *A Sound of Distant Drums.* A good money-maker."

"I'm glad to hear it. I'm always happy to see the arts prosper."

"You and me both, boy. What about Grildquist?"

"Can you do any checking on him for me? Have you got anybody relatively close to him?"

"In the theater, yes. But not at home. Unless maybe his chauffeur. I don't know, I'll have to check on that."

"Well, here's what I want to know. Where was he yesterday afternoon, particularly around four o'clock. What's his relationship with Mavis St. Paul recently, and does his ex-wife fit into the picture at all."

"Which wife? He's been married three times."

"Oh, Christ. The one he was married to four, five years ago. I'd also like to know where *she* was yesterday afternoon."

"I can't promise anything, Clay. Particularly with the wife. I might not know anybody who knows her. But I'll see what I can do."

"Thanks, Bull."

I hung up and checked names off my list. There were only two people left to cover, Ernest Tesselman and the husband from Illinois.

I wasn't sure whether I liked the idea of the husband from Illinois or not. Apparently, he and Mavis hadn't seen each other for five years at the very least. For him to all of a sudden come out of the past and kill her just didn't make too much sense.

On the other hand, there might be more to Mavis St. Paul's marriage than I knew about yet. And the first thing to do was to find out who Mavis St. Paul had been married to. Which meant I had to get in touch with somebody who was in touch with Belleville, Illinois.

Now, where the hell was Belleville, Illinois?

The way I figure it, if you want to find a small town, you find out what big town is near it. And when I think of Illinois, the big town I think of is Chicago.

So I wasted a long-distance phone call, to a guy I know in Chicago, who while not in Ed Ganolese's organization is in a somewhat similar organization with some of the same people on the board of directors.

"Belleville?" he repeated. "That's way the hell downstate, Clay. That isn't our territory at all."

"Fine," I said. "It isn't near Chicago."

"Hell no."

"So what is it near?"

"St. Louis," he said.

"St. Louis? That's in Missouri."

"Sure it is. It's on the Missouri side of the Mississippi River. Just across the river is East St. Louis, Illinois. Belleville is around there somewhere."

"East St. Louis, eh?"

"That's the place. They'll be able to help you down there. I don't know Belleville from Bellevue."

So I called East St. Louis. Some years back, the citizens of St. Louis made the mistake of electing a reform administration in their fair city, and all the rough-and-ready boys immediately moved across the river to East St. Louis. They're still there. And the citizens who did it to them now bitch about what a dull town St. Louis is, not like the wide-open town across the river, and the traffic on the bridges gets heavier every day.

So, as I say, I called East St. Louis, where there are also people I know and where there is also an organization similar in content and motives to the organization I work for. I called a guy who's named himself Tex, something he could never get away with in New York, and I said, "Tex, I'd like some information on a broad who used to live over in Belleville. That's near you, isn't it?"

"Sure," he said. "About fifteen miles from here, over toward the air base."

"It's nice to know it's really there," I said. "Here's the bit: Five, six years ago, a Belleville broad named Mary Komacki married somebody from the air base. I'd like to know who it was she married."

"How do you spell that name?"

I spelled it for him, and he said, "When I get it, where do I reach you?"

I gave him my phone number and said, "You can call collect, of course."

"Of course," he said. "What the hell do you think?"

Nice guy. I thanked him and hung up. That left one name on the list. Ernest Tesselman. I still liked him for the job, and I'd check on him myself.

And now it was time to go visiting. I looked in the telephone directory, and I found out where everybody lived, and I copied all the addresses down in my notebook. Then I went to the bedroom to put on a tie.

While I was there, the doorbell rang, and I figured

it almost inevitably had to be Grimes. I wondered who was dead this time, and I walked back through the apartment to the living room.

I figured it was Grimes, but it might be somebody else, so I checked the peephole before opening the door. And it's a good thing I did. The minute the peephole was open, he fired through it. The bullet took a layer of skin off my thumb knuckle before whizzing by my head and thunking into the opposite wall.

Chapter Thirteen

When I hear a shot, I hit the floor. If two years in the Army hadn't taught me that, nine years with Ed Ganolese had. So I spent a few seconds digging into the rug, until I realized that sound I was listening to was somebody running down the hall toward the elevator.

I scrabbled up to my feet and yanked the door open, just in time to see the elevator door slide shut. I didn't even get a glimpse of the guy. I ran down the hall and pressed the UP button a few times, but I knew it wouldn't do any good. The elevator wouldn't come back up for me until it had finished taking the cutie all the way downstairs. By the time it came back up, gathered me, and went back down again, he could be halfway across Jersey.

I went back down the hall and pulled my apartment door shut. I'd been planning to go out anyway, so I thought I might as well keep going. And while I was waiting for the elevator, I could spend a few seconds wondering just what the hell the shooting had been all about.

Then the great light dawned. I'd been in the papers, suspected of killing Betty Benson. The guy I was after must have read that, and realized he'd gotten to Betty

Benson too late, that I'd already been there, that whatever it was she had known I knew.

The elevator arrived and I stepped in and pushed the button for the main floor. I was going to go see everybody on my list of possible suspects. Somewhere along the line, I would be having a chat with a guy who had just tried to kill me.

Chapter Fourteen

I decided to try Johnny Ricardo first, not because he was my chief suspect, but because he was handiest. He had a supper club over on East 59th Street called, oddly enough, Johnny's Pub. I took a cab, leaving the Mercedes in its garage, since finding a parking space within a dozen blocks of Johnny's Pub at nine o'clock at night was something only a tourist would try for.

Johnny's Pub was divided in half. The front half was the bar, and the back half was the restaurant and also the place where the entertainment—folk singers and comics who imitate queers and other comics who imitate Mort Sahl or Orson Bean—was put on twice nightly.

I went on past the bar and into the restaurant-club part. I stood in the entranceway for a minute, in the semidark, looking at the people crowded around the tiny tables, and the maroon drapes hanging all over the place, and the desktop-size stage, empty at the moment, and then a waiter, black and white and funereal, sidled up and offered to show me where the tables were.

"I don't want to eat," I told him. "I want to talk to Johnny Ricardo."

His expression changed without seeming to, and he said, "I'm not sure he's in. Who's looking for him?"

"Tell him I'm from Ed Ganolese," I said, figuring

that name would mean more to him than my own. Johnny Ricardo and I, for some strange reason, had never had any dealings together before, though Johnny almost *had* to be linked with Ed Ganolese in one way or another.

"I'll see if he's in his office," said my friend. "If you'd care to wait in the bar—"

"That's okay," I said. "I'll wait here. Save you some steps."

He shrugged without seeming to shrug, and padded silently away. I hung around, looking at things, and after a while he came back and said, "He's in. Through the curtain over there and up the stairs. First door on your right."

"Thanks."

I followed directions, through the maroon curtain and up the maroon-carpeted stairs and through the maroon-painted first door on the right, and wound up in the office of Johnny Ricardo. After all the maroon outside, this place was practically invisible. It was gray, gray walls and gray carpet, gray filing cabinet and gray desk, gray drapes on the two windows and a gray wastebasket near a gray chair. Even the painting on the wall was done in varying shades of gray.

So was the guy behind the desk. Gray, just like his office and his suit, with a pale and bloodless and heavily lined face, washed-out hair and washed-out eyes, and gray bony hands sticking out of his gray coat sleeves.

The thin lips smiled as he got to his feet. "I'm Johnny Ricardo," he said, and his voice was gray too, hoarse and high. He stuck a skin-and-bones hand out, and I touched it carefully, trying not to break anything in it, and told him who I was.

He kept smiling. "You're from Ed Ganolese, you say."

"That's right."

"Well, I hope there isn't anything I can do for you. You know how it is." He was still smiling, but his eyes were wary. He motioned at the gray chair beside the desk. "Sit down."

"Thanks."

We both sat down, and he said, "What brings you here? It isn't going to cost me money, I hope."

I shook my head. "No, this isn't that kind of call. Nobody has any complaints about you that I know of."

"I'm glad to hear that," he said, but his eyes stayed wary, and his bony hands were clenching and unclenching on the arms of his chair.

"What I'm here about," I said, "is a girl you used to know. Mavis St. Paul. Maybe you remember her?"

"Mavis?" He looked puzzled, but managed to keep smiling anyway. "You meet so many girls in this business," he said. His eyes moved away from me, and he studied the painting on the wall. "Mavis," he said again. "Mavis St. Paul. That's an unusual name."

"Her stage name," I said.

"A singer?"

"No, an actress. I've heard she wasn't much as a singer."

"Mavis, Mavis—oh, my God, yes! Of course, of course, *Mavis!* Why, it's been three years if it's been a day!" He was looking at me again, surprised and pleased by the recollection of good old Mavis. "What in the world do you want to know about Mavis?" he asked me.

"Don't you keep up with the newspapers?"

"In this business?" He spread his hands wide and grinned wryly at me. "Not in this business, my friend. I live strictly non-normal hours, and most of my waking time is spent right here at this desk, or outside auditioning acts, keeping the bartenders' hands out of the till—I don't have time for newspapers or television or things like that."

"Then you don't know about Mavis?"

"Know what about her?"

I sidestepped that question. It's a gimmick the cops have tried to pull on me a couple of times. If he already knew the answer, he might forget I hadn't given it to him, and he just might mention it later in the conversation. So, instead of answering, I asked a question of my own: "How long's it been since you've seen her, do you remember?"

"Mavis? Oh, God, forever. I don't remember. Three years ago, anyway. She left me to play around with some clown from television. Martin or Morgan or something like that. We were just one of those crazy flings, like the fella says in the song. I knew she wouldn't be staying for very long, and she knew I wouldn't want her to stay very long. You know how it is."

I thought about Ella, and the string of chicks before Ella, and the difference that was Ella, and I said, "Yeah, I know how it is. But you haven't seen Mavis since she left you for this Morgan character?"

"Morgan, Martin, something like that. Started with an M. Had something to do with television."

"Yeah, but have you seen her at all since then?"

"Mavis? No, of course not. I don't know why she ever hooked up with me in the first place. She didn't want to break into the nightclub circuit. She was an actress, not an entertainer. And she couldn't sing a note."

"So I've heard. What was she like, anyway? What kind of a girl was she?"

He grinned at me. "Oh, she was a sharp girl," he said. "She knew what she wanted, that girl did."

"And what was it she wanted?"

"Money," he said. "That's all, just money. And lots of it."

"Was she really hipped on an acting career?"

"In a funny kind of a way. She figured that when you were an actress, you were famous. And she also figured that when you were famous you were rich. She couldn't visualize anybody being famous and poor. So she was hipped on it, but it goes right back to the main issue. She wanted cash, and plenty of it. She even put out for her drama teacher, way back when, so she could get her acting lessons free. A real miser, a real money-counter."

"Kind of grasping, huh?"

"Oh, hell, no. She was sweet about it all. Don't get me wrong, she wasn't one of these hard-eyed peroxide bitches, like the tramp I'm going with now. Not a bit of it. She was a real sweet kid, easy to get along with, lots of fun in the rack. You know. But she always kept one eye open for the dollar."

"How come you talk about her in the past tense?" I asked him. "Did she die or something?"

"Mavis? Not that I know of. She's around some-where, maybe still with that television type, whatever the hell his name was, though I doubt it. She's prob-ably lolling around on somebody's yacht right this minute, having the time of her life and sneaking a look at her bankbook every couple of minutes. No, I talk about her in the past tense because as far as I'm con-cerned she is in the past. She's in my past. Half an hour after you leave here, I'll talk about you in the past tense. That won't mean you're dead."

"I was just wondering," I said. Then I tried throwing him a curve, just to see what would happen. "What about Betty Benson?" I asked him.

"Who?" It looked like a legitimate double-take to me, though I'm not exactly an expert on double-takes.

"Betty Benson," I said.

He grinned some more. "Come on," he said. "No-body's named Betty Benson."

"This girl was."

He raised his eyebrows and kept on grinning. "Was?"

That had been a slip. I grinned sheepishly and said, "My past. I got the habit from you. She is. Named Betty Benson, I mean."

"Am I supposed to know this girl? Mavis, yes. But nobody named Betty Benson."

"I thought maybe you might have met her. She was— uh, *is*—a friend of Mavis's."

He thought about it for a minute, and then shook his head. "I'm afraid not," he said. "Mavis St. Paul I might forget for a minute. I mean, it's an unusual name, but what broad around New York doesn't have an unusual name? And it has been three years. But Betty Benson—if I ever met a chick named Betty Benson, I'd remember it."

"Yeah, I suppose so," I said.

"Why all this interest in Mavis, anyway?" he asked me. "She didn't get herself in trouble with the syndicate, did she?"

Syndicate is a word I don't use. I don't know what you think of when you hear the word syndicate, but I think of comic strips and advice-to-the-lovelorn columns and things like that. The people who distribute all that crap to newspapers all over the country are syndicates. The outfit I work for has nothing to do with advice for the lovelorn, except for maybe Archie Freihofer's department. I work for a company, an outfit, an organization. But not a syndicate.

But I didn't mention that to Ricardo. Instead, I said, "I'm not exactly sure what's up. I'm just an errand boy."

"I hope she isn't in trouble," he said.

"I don't suppose she is. What about her husband?"

He looked blank. "Husband?"

"I was told she'd gotten herself married before she came to New York."

"Beats me," he said. "I don't remember her ever mentioning it."

"Well," I said, getting to my feet, "thanks a lot for your time."

"Not at all," he said. "Just so it doesn't cost me money, I'll cooperate one hundred percent." He chuckled, a sound that belonged in a mausoleum. "Of course, if it cost me money, I'd only cooperate ninety percent. I need my margin of profit, you know."

"Yeah," I said. I started for the door, then stopped and went back to the desk again. "By the way," I said. "Do you have a gun?"

"What's that got to do with anything?"

"Nothing to do with Mavis," I said. "It was something else, I almost forgot all about it."

"Listen, I'll cooperate—"

"I was just wondering if you had a gun," I said.

"Well, of course I do. I keep large amounts of money in the safe here—"

"You don't have to justify it," I told him. "I was just wondering if you had one. Where is it, in your desk?"

"Yes. But I don't—"

"Could I see it for a second?"

"Listen," he said, and now he wasn't gray any more, he was pure white. "Listen, what is this? I haven't done anything to Ed Ganolese—"

"Stop being so worried," I said. "I don't want to use it on you. If I did, I'd pick a more private place than your club to do it. I just want to look at it for a second."

"Why?"

"I'm interested in guns."

I held my hand out, and he tried to stare me down, but I had Ed Ganolese and the whole organization staring on my side, and he finally looked away from me, shrugged his shoulders, and opened a desk drawer.

The gun he handed me was a monster, a Colt .45 automatic, the kind of gun that spreads people all over the landscape. "You expect to be robbed by elephants?" I asked him.

"A gun's a gun," he said, which wasn't exactly true, but I didn't argue with him. I sniffed at the barrel and didn't smell anything but cold metal. I took the clip out, and it was full. I broke it open, and it was clean and well greased. It hadn't been fired for some time.

"This the only gun you have?" I asked him.

"Yes," he said.

"Well, thanks again."

I gave him back his blockbuster, and he said, "Mavis is dead, isn't she? Was she shot, is that it? Who was she playing around with lately, Ed Ganolese?"

"You ought to read the papers more often," I told him.

Chapter Fifteen

Cy Grildquist was next, I decided, so I walked down the block from Johnny's Pub and stopped off at the drugstore on the corner to make a phone call. I wasn't sure whether a producer would normally be found at the theater during his show or at home. I tried the theater first, and they told me he wouldn't be in his office until the next afternoon. So I tried him at home.

He answered himself, a heavy-voiced individual, sounding as though he'd been smoking too many cigars too long. "This is Grildquist," he said, and waited for me to tell him who I was.

I didn't want to warn him in advance that somebody was coming over to talk to him about Mavis St. Paul, so I said, "I'm a playwright, Mr. Grildquist. I haven't had anything accepted yet, but—"

As I'd expected, he went immediately into the brush-off routine. "I'm sorry," he said. "I'm tied up with *A Sound of Distant Drums* right now, and I'm afraid I only look at plays submitted by agents. I'd suggest you go talk to an agent."

"Oh," I said. "Well, thanks a lot."

"Any time," he said.

I left the drugstore, hailed a cab, and went up to Grildquist's address, in the East 60's. Only four blocks from Mavis St. Paul's apartment, but in New York that doesn't mean a thing. A New York City apartment is like a home on the moon. For all intents and purposes there isn't anybody else around for a million miles.

Grildquist's building was just off Fifth Avenue and the park, and I could see right away it wasn't going to be an easy place to get into. There was a doorman and, behind him, a small telephone switchboard setup attached to the wall. Before I could get by the doorman, somebody in that building was going to have go give the okay.

Well, I was going to have to give Cy Grildquist advance warning, after all. I walked up to the entrance, the doorman held the door open for me, and I went on in.

The doorman said, "Who did you wish to see, please?"

"Mr. Grildquist," I said.

"Your name?"

"Tell him I'm from Ernest Tesselman," I said, hoping Grildquist knew who Ernest Tesselman was. "It's about Mavis."

"Mavis?"

"That's right."

"And your own name, sir?"

"Just say I'm from Ernest Tesselman," I repeated.

He thought it over for a few seconds, then shrugged and went away to his switchboard. I waited, looking around at the shining tile and marble of the lobby, and then the doorman came back to me and said, "Eleven C, sir. Take the first elevator."

I thanked him, and took the first elevator. Eleven C

was just across the hall from the elevator, and Grildquist opened the door the minute I pressed the bell
button.

He had to be Grildquist. He went with that cigar-
smoker's voice. Heavy, florid, well jowled, prosperous
and paunchy, dressed in a slightly old-fashioned brown
suit, complete with vest and ultraconservative tie.

He told me to come in and led the way to the living
room, where he told me to sit down. He then asked me
if I wanted something to drink. I mentioned Scotch
and water, and he went away to mix it while I looked at
the room.

Broadway producing apparently pays off. The living
room was huge, and on two levels. Midway across, two
steps led down to a sunken area in the room, where a
white sofa, white rug and white tables blended rather
nicely with pale-green walls, dark-wood bar and con-
sole, and rough-tile fireplace. The fireplace looked real,
though there was no fire going in it at the moment.
French doors led out from this part of the living room
to a terrace and the lights of the city.

The upper part of the living room, where I was sitting, was dominated by an overgrown color television
set. Armchairs and sofas were placed here and there,
their position determined entirely by the position of
the television set. It was impossible to sit down anywhere in the room without having that huge blank
screen staring you in the face. I wished I could move
down to the non-electronic half of the room.

Grildquist came back with drinks, handed me mine,
and sat down off to my left. We drank a bit and looked

at the blank television screen. Then Grildquist said, in a casual tone of voice, as though it wasn't very important, "Who is Ernest Tesselman?"

"Mavis's last boyfriend," I said. I looked over at him. "You let me up here without knowing who Tesselman was?"

He smiled at the television set. "You thought that was the magic name? No, I'm sorry. The name Mavis was what opened the door for you."

"Oh," I said. "I see."

He was still looking at the television set, so I did, too. But it was still off. For some reason, that set slowed the conversation down to a crawl. Grildquist and I weren't looking at each other, we were looking at the TV. We weren't talking to each other, we were talking to that big square idiot-face, and the set was translating or something.

"Thing broke down a couple of weeks ago," Grildquist said suddenly. "The hell with it. I never watch it anyway. My wife was the television fan."

"That's your competition, isn't it?" I asked him.

"No," he said. "People watch television when they don't feel like exerting themselves to find something good. When they want something good, they go to the theater. Television and theater are competitors the same way flat beer and good Scotch are competitors."

"This is fine Scotch," I said, tinkling the ice cubes against the glass.

"Thank you," he said. "You were the playwright who called a while back, weren't you?"

"I wanted to know if you were home."

"I take it you're a private detective," he said.

"Like on television? No, I'm afraid not. Just a friend of Ernest Tesselman's."

"Mavis's last boyfriend."

"That's right."

"Don't say anything for a minute," he said. "Let me make a few guesses." He adjusted himself in his chair, frowned gloomily at the television set, and said, "Your Mr. Tesselman doesn't think the man the police are after is really the one who killed Mavis. So he hired you, or asked you, or told you, depending on your relationship with him, to nose around and find out who the killer really is. You nosed around, as per instructions, and somebody or other told you I used to know Mavis. That made me a suspect. So you've come up here to find out whether or not I murdered her."

"And you were expecting me," I told the TV. "Why?"

"As a matter of fact, I wasn't. But a theatrical producer spends a large portion of his life reading plays. A great many of them are mysteries. In addition, there's—" He gestured at the television. "When the doorman told me someone wanted to talk to me about Mavis, it was easy to see I was cast as a character in Act Two, Scene One."

"Why did you let me come on up?"

"If I turned you away, you'd be convinced I was the man you were after. I'm not particularly busy this evening, and a short conversation with you can't do any harm. Besides, it might help you, though I admit I can't see how. But I'd like the killer found. Mavis was a good girl."

"I've been told she was mercenary," I said, remembering Betty Benson's description.

He laughed. "Not completely," he said. "That's a fairly accurate description of Mavis's personality, but I'm afraid it's misleading. Mavis wasn't a whore, she wouldn't go to bed with just any man who had the money. She had to like a man before she'd pay any attention to him."

"And she only liked rich men," I said.

"That was a phase, I think. I think she would have matured out of it. It was just a reaction to that marriage of hers."

"Marriage?"

"You must have heard she was married once."

"Back in her home town."

"Yes. A professional man of some kind. A bright, steady future of the suburban ranch-style variety. He offered her security and love, rather than wealth, and then he deserted her. So she didn't want security and love any more. She wanted wealth. It was understandable."

"What was her married name, do you know?"

"Wasn't it St. Paul? No, I suppose that was a stage name, come to think of it. I'm sorry, I don't think she ever mentioned the man's name. She didn't like to talk about him."

"How did you happen to meet her in the first place?"

"Paul Devon brought her to a party. He's an acting teacher, also done some directing, off-Broadway. They'd been going together for a while."

"And you were richer," I said.

He smiled at the television set. "That takes care of my manly charm, doesn't it? I suppose you're right. I was richer. I was also a Broadway producer, and Mavis wanted desperately to be a star."

"Did she have any talent?"

"Some. Not enough, really. She was too sporadic, her interpretations were always too shallow."

"Why did you split up?"

"My wife was planning on divorcing me. I thought it would be better if I trod the straight and narrow for a while, rather than give my wife ammunition. By the time that was all over with, Mavis was off with somebody else. A nightclub man, I think."

"What was your attitude about that?"

"I got another girl." He looked away from the television set long enough to grin at me. "I bore Mavis no ill will," he said. "Besides, that was more than three years ago."

"Have you seen her since then?"

"Once or twice, at parties. We were still friends, but we didn't see much of one another."

"When was the last time you saw her?"

"Well over a year ago. She was with Charlie Morgan, a television producer. He died shortly after that."

"Have you seen Betty Benson lately?"

"Benson?" He frowned, studying the TV. "Benson," he said again. "Oh, you mean Mavis's friend. The hometowny little girl." He looked over at me suddenly. "Is that the girl who was just killed?"

"That's right."

"You think it's the same man, of course."

"Of course."

"I only met the girl once. Before Mavis moved into the apartment I rented for her. I barely remember what she looked like."

"And you've never seen her since."

"No, I've had no need to."

"Do you own a gun?"

He looked at me again, puzzled. "Mavis was stabbed, wasn't she?"

"So was Betty Benson," I said. "I was just wondering if you owned a gun."

"As a matter of fact, I do. It isn't really mine, it belonged to my second wife."

"The one you were married to while you were going with Mavis?"

"Yes. She left it here, and I never got around to giving it back to her. She's out in California now, and I believe there are some laws about shipping guns in the mail."

"Could I see it?"

"Could I ask why?"

"Somebody took a shot at me tonight."

"Oh." He got to his feet. "I'm not sure I can find it," he said.

"I would like to look at it."

"How strong a suspect am I?" he asked suddenly.

"I don't have any rating system set up," I told him.

"If I don't find the gun, I imagine I'll become more of a favorite," he said.

"That depends," I said.

"I'll take a look for it. Mix yourself another drink while I'm gone."

"Thanks."

He went away, and I got to my feet, refusing to look at the television set. Grildquist's glass was empty, too, so I carried them both down to the lower part of the living room and made new drinks. Then I went back and sat down again, but the television set was growing increasingly annoying, so I got up and shifted my chair so it faced the one Grildquist was sitting in. I shifted his chair, too, sat back down again, and Grildquist came back.

He had the gun in his hand, a little .25, shiny-barreled, ivory-handled, a ladies' gun, the kind advertised as being "handy for pocket or purse." He was holding it loosely, but his finger was touching the trigger. The barrel was aimed at a point on the floor midway between us.

He stood in the doorway for a second, half-smiling at me. Then he said, "You know, if I were the man who'd killed Mavis and who'd tried to kill you, you'd be in an awkward position right now. I could shoot you, chop your body up in the bathtub, and drop the pieces down the incinerator."

"Did that come out of one of the plays you read?" I asked him.

"Yes," he said. His smile broadened. "I rejected it. Unrealistic. The private detective wouldn't get himself into a position like this."

"The doorman knows I came up," I said.

"Why should he remember you? Why should he ever wonder where you went?"

"Mr. Tesselman knows I was coming here."

"Did he know you got here?"

"If you're kidding," I told him, "you're taking your life in your hands."

"Why? I'm the one with the gun."

"If I move fast enough, you might miss the first time."

He frowned. "The joke is going sour," he said, and walked over to hand me the gun.

I took it from him, smelled the barrel, broke it open. It was empty, and it had been neither fired nor cleaned in some time. I gave it back. "You shouldn't joke with guns," I said.

"I suppose not." He sat down, glanced over at the television set, looked back at me. "You moved the chairs."

There was no sense answering that one. "About your second wife," I said. "Did she ever meet Mavis?"

"I certainly hope not. No, I don't think so, or she would have said something about it. Janeen wasn't the silent type."

"You say she's in California now?"

"Married again. Why, did you think she might have had an attack of belated jealousy? Janeen isn't a murderess, at least not with a knife. Her method is to talk people to death."

"You had a third wife, didn't you?"

"She's in Europe. And I had been finished with Mavis for some time before I even met Alisan."

I worked at my drink for a minute, and then said, "I can't think of any more questions. Can you think of any more answers?"

He smiled over his drink. "I can think of a couple of questions," he said. "For instance, you haven't mentioned your name. Or your connection with this Mr. Tesselman."

I finished my drink. "You're right," I said, getting to my feet. "I never did. Thank you for your time."

"I would like to know," he said.

I smiled at him and started for the door.

"Would it do any good," he asked me, "for me to threaten you with the police?"

I stopped and looked back at him. "In what way?"

"I could call the doorman after you leave here, tell him to stop you from getting out of the building. Then I could call the police and tell them you impersonated a detective."

"Why would you want to do that?"

"You've had this whole thing your way," he said. "I'm not used to that. I want to know who you are."

"Do you know anybody named Bull Rocco?" I asked him.

"Union man?"

"That's him. Did he ever give you a bad time for any reason?"

"No, I've gotten along with him all right. I haven't had an awful lot to do with him. Why?"

"If you give me a bad time," I told him, "Bull will give you a bad time."

"You're the damnedest name-dropper I've ever met," he said. "Any minute now, you'll tell me you also know George Clayton."

I gaped at him. "George Clayton?"

"That was the man arrested for killing the Benson girl. Don't tell me you don't know him."

I grinned at him and relaxed. I'd forgotten about the newspapers. Of course my full name had gone in. "I *am* him," I said.

He didn't believe me.

Chapter Sixteen

I still had three people to see, Alan Petry and Paul Devon and Ernest Tesselman, but I decided they could wait till tomorrow. It was now after ten o'clock at night, and it would be easier to get in to talk to people in the daytime. I had four hours to kill until I was due to pick up Ella at the Tambarin, so I went back home.

I was just finishing a beer when the phone rang. I hadn't expected anybody to come through with information this fast, and I tried to figure out who'd be calling me, as I went into the living room and picked up the phone.

It was a voice I didn't recognize, deep and muffled and heavily accented. "You are Clay?" it asked.

"Who's calling?"

"Do you know," asked this voice, the words all garbled by the accent, "a Mr. William Cantell?"

"William Cantell? Do you mean Billy-Billy Cantell?"

"That is him. He has asked me to telephone you."

"When did he ask this?"

"Just a few moments ago."

"You know where he is?"

"He asked me," said the voice, maddeningly slow and almost impossible to understand because of the accent, "to tell you where you might meet him."

"Where?" I asked, fumbling for pencil and paper.

"There is a tube station at 95th Street—"

"A what?"

"Your pardon. A subway station. It is no longer in use. Mr. Cantell is there now, waiting for you."

"In a subway station?"

"Do you have pencil and paper? I will tell you how to get there."

"Yes, go ahead."

"Now, listen," he said. "This subway station is no longer in use. The normal entrances have been sealed off. But there is still a way to get into the station, through the cellar of a building on East 95th Street." He gave me instructions on getting into the subway station, and I copied them down. Then he said, "The authorities are using the platforms for the storage of lumber and other building materials. Mr. Cantell has fashioned himself a little hideaway on the downtown platform. Do you have that? On the platform where trains going downtown would stop. That is on the west side of the station."

"I have it," I said.

"You must go across the overpass to the downtown platform," he said, "and then turn left. He is down at the southern end of the platform. He has taken refuge behind a stack of lumber there. Do you have all that?"

"I have all that," I said. "What did you say your name was?"

"Mr. Cantell told me," he said, "that it would be unnecessary for me to give my name, since you do not know me."

"I'd like to know you," I said, and the phone clicked in my ear as he hung up.

I sat there for a while, trying to decide what to do. I didn't believe for a minute that this guy was anybody but my cutie. The phony foreign accent, the use of Billy-Billy as bait. He wanted to get me into a nice quiet spot where he could finish the job he'd loused up earlier in the evening.

Well, I'd give him his chance. I didn't doubt I'd find my cutie waiting for me in that unused subway station. And it was nice to know, for a change, just where the guy was.

I went back out into the heat, walked down to the garage, and got the Mercedes from the Puerto Rican kid. "Still hot," he told me, as he got out of the car.

"Have a good sleep in the movies?"

"Pretty good. You been thinkin' about me for a job?"

"It isn't what you think it is, kid," I told him.

He shrugged. "It's better than workin' here," he said.

"That's what you think."

"I wanna get out of here."

"I'll ask around," I told him. "I don't promise anything."

"Thanks, mister," he said. "You tell them, I drive like hell. And when cops ask me questions, I don't speak English."

"I'll tell them," I said.

I got behind the wheel of the Mercedes, said so long to the kid, who was grinning from ear to ear, and drove up to 86th Street and through the park to the East Side. On the way, I pulled out the .32 from under the dashboard, and checked it. It was clean and loaded and ready to go. I slipped it into my suitcoat pocket.

I found a parking space a couple of doors away from the house I wanted. This was a quasi-tenement block, brick buildings four and five stories high, built to be cheap apartment buildings. They hadn't depreciated, because they'd never been anything particularly good. But they were still half a notch above real tenements, and the smell was still bearable.

I walked into the hall of the building I wanted, hunted around for a minute, and found the cellar door. It was locked, but the lock was one of those old-fashioned things, and I have the two standard skeleton keys on my key chain. The first one I tried opened the door. I slipped through, shut the door behind me, and switched on the light. A million cockroaches went scurrying off the steps and walls, ducking into cracks and crannies. I went down the stairs and headed cautiously for the rear of the building. I expected to find the cutie in the station itself, but he just might be waiting here in the cellar.

The break in the wall was right where he'd said it would be. I crawled through, picked my way over some ancient rubble, and wound up on the subway platform. A few small electric bulbs were the only illumination.

This was one of the really old-time subway stations, shaped like the interior of a Quonset hut, with a high-domed curving ceiling covered with mosaic tile in patterns too complicated for today's hurrying builders to bother with. A rickety-looking metal overpass stretched high over the tracks, leading to the other platform. Stacks of lumber and other building materials, as the cutie had said, covered about half the floor area of both platforms. The cutie could be waiting behind any of them.

I dragged the .32 out of my pocket and inched forward, heading for the overpass. I went up the steps, slow and cautious and moving in a half-crouch, and just got to the top when a rumbling down to my left told me a train was coming.

I didn't want any subway motorman to get a look at me. If one did, he'd call in to the dispatcher's office, and the place would be crawling with cops in no time. Besides that, I didn't relish the idea of being spotlighted by the train's headlamps. I'd make too good a target for the cutie to shoot at. So I threw myself flat on the steel floor of the overpass and waited for the train to go by.

There were two of them, one northbound and one southbound, and they went by simultaneously, with racket enough to ruin my eardrums for life. I waited one long minute after they'd both gone by, and then I got slowly to my feet and moved forward again, still in the half-crouch.

I went down the steps on the other side, and waited again. Somewhere down in the lumber-filled and tarpaulin-mounded dimness to my left, Billy-Billy was supposed to be waiting for me. Sure. Well, *something* was waiting for me down there. If I was right, it was the guy who'd killed Mavis St. Paul.

I headed down in that direction, moving slowly and cautiously from one stack of lumber to the next. I'd never before realized just how long subway platforms really are. I was about halfway to the end when I heard another train coming. I knelt behind a tarpaulin-covered mound, and waited. In a minute, two trains roared through again, the row of lighted windows flashing by and throwing fast patterns of light and darkness on the wall behind me. The last car of the northbound train threw a blinding blue-white spark out just as it passed the station, and for a millisecond the whole place was etched clear and bright.

Then it was quiet and dark again, and I moved on. I hadn't heard a sound so far, except for my own muffled movements and the passage of the trains. I wondered if this was just somebody's bad idea of a joke.

I finally got down to the end of the platform, and there was the last stack of lumber, directly in front of me. I sidled up to the edge of it, shoved the .32 out in front of me, and peeked around the lumber.

And the joke was on me, because there, right there in front of me, eyes wide open and looking at me, sat Billy-Billy Cantell.

But the joke was on Billy-Billy, too. He was dead.

Chapter Seventeen

I stood there, crouched, for a long minute, just staring at him. He'd been knifed. There was a jagged cut across his filthy shirt front, now filthier than ever, smeared with dried blood. A series of brownish ribbons ran down his shirt front and connected with a dry brown pool on the cement floor, beside his left hand.

He had been brought here, and then he had been knifed. The amount of blood on the floor by the left hand (that left hand, palm up, fingers curled, pale and lifeless, the very expression of death) showed that he hadn't been brought here after he'd been murdered.

I stood there, staring at him, and then sound brought me back to movement and awareness again. Sound, the sound of voices. I straightened, tense and listening. The voices were coming from the black maw of the subway tunnel, from down to the south of me.

And then I saw it, I saw what the killer had suckered me into. He'd called me and sent me up here to find Billy-Billy. And then he'd called the police and told *them* Billy-Billy was here. The way he'd had it all doped out, the law would not only find Cantell, they would also find me.

It didn't matter whether or not the cops could pin the Cantell killing on me. They wouldn't have to. I

work for Ed Ganolese. I work for an organization outside the law, and the law doesn't have to wait around to
get me on a murder rap. The law will grab me on any
rap it can find.

My being down here, in this closed and abandoned
subway station, was illegal already, a nice cheap conviction, and the law would jump at the chance to grab
me for it. The .32 in my hand was another cheap conviction. The law could put me away for a few years without
bringing in the Cantell killing at all. And there goes the
cutie, scot-free.

I had to get the hell out of there. I turned and ran.
I wasn't worried about noise now, all I was worried
about was getting out of that station and out of that
neighborhood.

I ran to the overpass and up the iron steps, and they
clanged beneath my feet. I heard sudden shouting way
down to my right, but I didn't waste time looking down
there. I raced across to the other side of the tracks and
down the steps, three at a time, and I dove through the
crumbled place in the wall and into the stinking cellar
of the quasi-tenement.

I stumbled over something or other getting through,
and sprawled on the cellar floor. I heard the .32 go
skittering away in the darkness. I had to find it, it had
my prints all over it. I scrabbled frantically through the
dust and refuse of the cellar floor, hearing the shouts
and the sound of running feet behind me, and at last
my fingers touched the barrel of the gun. I picked it
up, got to my feet, and ran for the stairs. I dashed up

the steps, ignoring the cockroaches scurrying around my feet, and shoved through the door to the hallway.

A short fat woman, lugging a grocery-filled shopping bag (at eleven-thirty at night!), was just passing the cellar door, and she gaped at me, all wide eyes and stained teeth. I slammed the door behind me, ignoring her, and pawed through my pockets for my keys. Then I realized I was still holding the .32, and that that was what the fat woman was staring pop-eyed at. I shoved it into my jacket pocket, found my keys, and locked the cellar door again. Already, I could hear feet pounding up the stairs.

I pushed by the fat woman, still gaping at me but not yet screaming, and ran out to the street.

Once I hit the pavement, I forced myself to stop running. I forced myself to stroll down to the Mercedes, to look casual and calm and peaceful, like an insurance salesman, and I got into the Mercedes, stuck the key into the ignition, and got the hell out of there.

All the way home, I thought about that bastard. First, he tries to kill me. When that doesn't work, he tries to set me up for a medium-size jail term, enough to keep me out of circulation for a few years. He knows me, and I don't know him, which means he has the edge on me. And it's no longer a case of the hunter and the hunted. We're both hunting now, and he has the edge on me.

And he isn't moving slowly. He's sniping away at me, one thing after the other, and he isn't going to slow down until he gets me.

Which means my next move is plain. I have to speed up. I have to work faster than he does, because I've got to make up for the edge he has on me. He knows who I am. I've got to know who he is.

Otherwise I'm dead.

Chapter Eighteen

I went home and left the Mercedes out front, by the sign that says TOW-AWAY ZONE. It was ten minutes to twelve, and parking is legal after midnight. If the cops could get a tow truck here within ten minutes, they were welcome to the car.

Upstairs, I went directly to the bathroom and looked at myself in the mirror. Oh, I was pretty. My face was filthy, with smudges of dirt on my forehead and right cheek and jaw, all of it running with perspiration. My hands were even dirtier than my face, and my clothes were a total loss. My shirt and jacket were both dirt-stained, and both knees of my trousers were ripped, probably from when I'd catapulted through into that cellar. A chunk of leather had been scraped away from the toe of my right shoe.

The cutie now owed me a clothing bill. I was looking forward to collecting.

I stripped, showered, put on clean clothes, and called Ed. I filled him in up to date, including the finding of Billy-Billy's body, and when I was finished, he said, "That rotten son of a bitch."

"Just what I was thinking," I said.

"Okay," said Ed. "Okay, okay. He asked for it. He went a little too far this time, Clay, he got a little too cute for his own good. The cops have Billy-Billy now, and that means they'll close the goddam case. That means he's ours, Clay. That son of a bitch is ours, we don't have to turn him over to the law at all."

"That's right," I said. "I hadn't thought about that."

"Neither did he, the bastard. But *I'm* thinking about it. Clay, I want that son of a bitch more than ever now. I want him right in front of me. He's mine, Clay. You get him and you deliver him to me. That little cutie has got just a bit too goddam cute for his own good."

"I'll get him, Ed," I promised.

"I'm counting on you, boy."

"Ed, listen, one more thing. This settles the Mavis St. Paul killing as far as the cops are concerned. But what about the Betty Benson thing? I'm still on the books for that one, you know."

"Now the cops have Billy-Billy," he said, "it shouldn't take too much work to convince them to use him for both jobs."

"I hope so. And what about Billy-Billy himself? You think the cops will be looking for the guy who killed him?"

"Hell, no. They'll figure it was us that did it, and they'll let it alone. What the hell do they care who bumped a little no-account punk like that?"

"Yeah, I guess so. Okay, Ed, I just thought you ought to know about Billy-Billy. I'll get back to work now."

"You do that, Clay. You bring me that bastard."

"On a platter," I said. "With an apple in his mouth."

"Hold on a second," he said. "Clancy ought to know about this, too. He's the guy to convince them to switch the Benson killing from you to Billy-Billy. You go out and talk to him, figure out some way to clear you, so they can use Billy-Billy."

"Out where? To his house?"

"Where the hell else? It's midnight."

"That's what I mean, Ed. You know how Clancy is about mixing his business life with his private life."

"Who isn't? The hell with that," he said. "This is important. You go on out and talk to him."

"Okay, Ed."

"Then get me the guy."

"Will do."

I shrugged into a jacket and was just about to leave, when the phone rang. It was Bull Rocco. "You wanted to know where Cy Grildquist was yesterday afternoon at four o'clock," he said. "I found out. At a backer's audition for his new play."

"For sure?" I asked him. "He couldn't have ducked out for maybe half an hour?"

"Not from a backer's audition. He was there for sure, sucking after money every minute."

"Thanks," I said. "Thanks a lot."

So now I knew one guy who was *not* the cutie I was looking for. That was nice.

Chapter Nineteen

Clancy Marshall lives in the Bronx, but not in the *Daily News* Bronx, the one people automatically think of when they hear the name. He lives farther north than that, still in the Bronx, still in a borough of New York City, but it's another world entirely. The section is called Riverdale, and it's neatly split between asterisk-shaped red-brick apartment buildings, seven to ten stories high, and winding country lanes flanked by ranch-style split-levels and solid prewar-style clap-boards with front porches, dining rooms, and attics. And it's all part of New York.

Clancy lived in one of the prewar clapboards, two stories high, painted white with green shutters and gray flooring on the porch. The front lawn was dotted with tiny statues, all in color. There were rabbits, pup-pies, frogs and ducks, all just as cute as morning televi-sion, and a plantation slave stereotype boy next to the carriage light, dressed in jockey's duds and with his black wooden hand permanently out to accept the reins. This is as close as some people can get to admit-ting they wish there was still an aristocracy.

I turned off Kingsbridge Road onto Rogers Lane, followed the curvature for a while, and pulled to a stop in front of Clancy's place. My Mercedes doesn't have any reins, so I shrugged at the plantation boy, his hand out in unflagging hope that a set of reins would some day once again be placed there, and clopped up the stoop to the front porch. It was now one o'clock in the morning, and only one upstairs window showed light. I knew Clancy wasn't going to be happy about this, but I rang the bell anyway. He could bitch at Ed, if he wanted.

It took me a while to get an answer, and then it was Clancy's wife, Laura. Laura Marshall is easily described. It only takes four words. She's a rich bitch suburban matron. She's the Congressional Whip, at the grass-roots level. Whip of the PTA, whip of the Junior League and the Monday Afternoon Club, whip of Clancy Marshall. She's a snob, and as far as she's concerned she's married to a well-to-do lawyer of the stuffy stocks-and-bonds corporation type. I don't mean she doesn't know what Clancy really does for a good living, but she manages pretty successfully to double-think herself into being able to spend his ill-gotten gains with no conscience tweaks.

Clancy, for some reason known only to Clancy, is madly in love with this well-girdled symptom of our times, and is deathly afraid that one of these days she's going to pack up and go away, her and the kiddies, of which there are two, inevitably two. (It isn't possible to have two point six.) Not that he doubts his own charm so much, he's just afraid that the dirt of his business will one day become so noticeable that Laura won't be able to ignore it any more. Then she'll leave. She probably will, too. Clancy doesn't do anything for her that a monthly alimony check couldn't do with less talk.

Most people who don't know me assume, on first seeing me, that I'm a rising young man in some business concern somewhere, maybe advertising or insurance or some such thing. In a way, that's almost true. But Laura Marshall, on seeing me at her door at one in the morning, obviously made the immediate decision that I couldn't possibly know anyone she knew, not on a social level at any rate, and she froze me with a glance, as the Victorians used to say.

The hell with her. I don't freeze that easy. "I'd like to speak to Clancy," I said, using the first name just to see her wince.

"At one o'clock in the morning?" she asked me.

"It's necessary," I said, and that's the closest I intended to get to an apology.

"My husband has office hours," she started, but I interrupted her. I didn't have all that much time. "Tell him Clay is here," I said. "He'll want to see me."

She looked as though she doubted it. "Wait here," she said, and closed the door in my face.

So I waited. There was a glider on the porch, one of those old green jobs, and I sat down on it. It squeaked, as I'd known it would, and I rocked back and forth, making noise for the fun of it. I wanted to irritate Laura Marshall just as much as her very existence irritated me.

Clancy pulled open the front door a couple minutes later. He was wearing a George Sanders robe, dark-colored, figure-patterned, shiny-lapeled, and his smile, in a less spineless man, could have been called dangerous. "Come in, Mr. Clay," he said. "We can talk in the study."

I followed him into the house. The study was off the dining room which was off the living room which was off the foyer by the front door. The whip was nowhere in sight.

In the study, a squarish room from *Better Homes and Gardens,* in which the celebrities used to show Ed Murrow their souvenirs, Clancy switched on the lights, shut the door, and turned to me to say, "Where the hell did you get the idea you could come here?" His voice was soft, but hard, and his usual fund-raising smile had been replaced by a furious glare.

"From Ed," I told him. "He not only told me I *could,* he told me I *should.* Things have been happening."

"You don't come to my house," he said. "Get that straight, for once and for all, you do not come to my house."

"I do when it's important."

He ignored that. "I told Laura you worked for a client of mine," he said. "A legitimate client. This is a business matter, and when you leave you talk that way."

"All right, all right. Let's get to the subject."

"The subject is that you don't come here," he insisted. "Not at all. I don't ever want you near this house again."

I wondered if I would some day be hiding from Ella that way. "Bitch at Ed, if you feel like bitching," I told him, pushing the thought of Ella out of my mind. "I've got more important things to do."

"I want it understood," he said. "You don't come

here. I have an office, and I'm in it all day long. This could wait for morning, whatever it is."

"Ed told me to come here. I don't want to argue about it. After letting me sit around in that lousy jail for nineteen hours, you're in no position to complain about anything I do to you."

"It was tough to get you out. They didn't want to let you go."

"Crap. You were sitting on your hands. That's a habit of yours. Sit down, for God's sake, and let's get to the subject at hand. I've got other things to do tonight."

He wanted to carry on about his home being his castle some more, but it finally got through to him that he wasn't getting anywhere that way. So he sat scowling behind his desk—as bare a desk as Ernest Tesselman's, but not as big—and I sat in the chair facing him.

"What is it?" he asked me. "Let's get it done and over with."

"I found Billy-Billy tonight," I told him. "So did the cops. They almost found us together."

His eyebrows rose, and he forgot to be sore at me. "The police have him? Or do you?"

"They do."

"So you want him out. Clay, you could have called me on that, you didn't have to come all the way up here."

"Shut up and listen for a second, Clancy. Billy-Billy was dead when I found him. All the cops have is the mortal coil, so to speak."

"Dead?" He sat back for a second, thinking that one over, and then he smiled at me. "Then it's all over," he said. "We can get back to normalcy now."

"I'm afraid not. Ed still wants me to find the guy for him."

"Why? For God's sake, if the police have Cantell's body, they'll be satisfied. The whole thing's finished."

"Ed isn't satisfied. We've been to a lot of trouble, and Ed wants the guy who caused it all."

He leaned over the desk toward me, anxious and sincere, all lawyer now, the husband forgotten. "Clay, listen," he said. "This is no way to run the business. Take it from me, Clay. For the last couple of days, we've been attracting attention to ourselves, we've been running into police trouble, and that is no way to keep a healthy organization."

"Tell Ed that, not me. I just follow orders."

"I intend to tell him. Where is he, home?"

"Uh huh. But I don't think you'll get anywhere with him. He's annoyed."

"I'm his lawyer, Clay. I've got to warn him when he's planning to do something stupid. And having you play Sherlock Holmes is stupid. You'll be bumping into people outside the organization, annoying them, bringing the cops back into it again, keeping the organization out where they can look at it and be reminded of it. Billy-Billy Cantell is dead, the police have the body. So the case is closed."

"The Betty Benson case isn't closed," I reminded him. "In fact, that's the main reason I'm here."

"I can square that with no problem at all," he told me. "They can use Billy-Billy for both killings. And they won't try very hard to find out who killed him. So the whole thing is finished. Let it stay finished, that's what I say."

"As I say, I'm not the one to talk to."

"I'll talk to Ed," he said. He said it very firmly, and I knew he'd have to spend some time building up his courage before he'd be able to call Ed Ganolese and tell him he's doing things wrong.

But that wasn't my concern. "Back to Betty Benson," I said. "I was there, I talked with her, I drank coffee, I left fingerprints all over the place. They have a half-hour spread on the time of the killing, and I've already admitted I was there during part of that time."

"She was alive when you left, that's all."

"How do I prove it?"

"What time did you leave the apartment?"

"Just about four o'clock. She was killed sometime between four and four-thirty. I've admitted to leaving at four."

"All right. Where did you go from there?"

"Straight home. The kid at the parking garage can tell what time I got there. They keep a record of times in and out on the cars kept there."

"Fine. A survey called her at four-fifteen, and she was still alive then. I can arrange that. Did she have a television set?"

"I didn't see one in the living room."

"All right. Her answer was, 'I'm sorry, but I don't

have a TV.' That was at four-fifteen. I can have that set up by ten o'clock in the morning. Then we drop a hint that Cantell actually did that killing, too, and you're off the hook."

"Why did he kill her? He didn't even know her. I'm not so sure the cops will go for this."

"Only he could tell why he did it, and unfortunately he's dead." Clancy flashed that charming smile of his at me. He was being the brilliant mouthpiece now, and loving every second of it. He went big for alibis and complex series of events so confusing that after a while nobody in the world would be able to work back to the truth. That's what made him so good in a courtroom.

"If you think you can do it," I said.

"I can do it. In the morning. You could have come to the office at nine."

"Ed told me to see you right away."

"Ed is getting too excited about this. If there's nothing else—"

"Nothing," I said. I got to my feet and said, "I'm Mr. Clay, is that it?"

"Robert Clay," he told me. "You work for Craig, Harry and Bourke."

"Good for me."

He walked me to the front door, talking loudly about the affairs of Craig, Harry and Bourke, whoever they are, and he went out on the front porch with me, closing the door behind him. "Sorry I got upset, Clay," he whispered. The smile clicked on like a neon sign, and he gave me a friendly pat on the arm. "I just don't like to bring my business home with me. Laura, you know."

"I know. I'll see you, Clancy." Ella wouldn't be like Laura, I was telling myself. Ella wouldn't be like Laura.

"I'll talk to Ed about stopping this nonsense," he said. "We shouldn't waste time playing cops and robbers."

"Not as cops, anyway," I told him.

Chapter Twenty

I knew Clancy wouldn't get anywhere with Ed. Ed wanted to get his hands on the guy who'd started all this trouble, and that was all there was to it. After the try to gun me, and the attempt to set me up at the subway station, I was kind of interested in finding the guy myself.

When I got back to the apartment, it was a little after one-thirty in the morning. I was supposed to pick Ella up at the Tambarin at two. I left the Mercedes out front and went upstairs to hang around for fifteen minutes.

The phone rang as I was taking off my coat. It was Fred Maine. "About Alan Petry," he said. "I couldn't find out anything about his home life at all, but I can tell you where to find him. He works a night beat on the West Side, in the Forties."

"Prowl car?"

"No, he walks. It's a two-man beat. I'm sorry, Clay, but I couldn't get anything at all, otherwise. I don't know the guy personally."

"Thanks, anyway," I said. "He's working now?"

"Yeah, I guess so. Unless it's his night off."

"Okay, thanks."

The West 40's. There was a bar on 46th Street, between Eighth and Ninth, where some of Archie

Freihofer's girls wait for phone calls. The boss there probably knew the cops working his beat. I took a chance on it and called the place.

A little Puerto Rican chick answered the phone, one of those cute-as-a-button voices. I told her I wanted to talk to the bartender, Alex, and she said, "Isn't there anything *I* can do for you?"

"I'm sure there is," I said. "But right now I want to talk to Alex."

"Who's calling?"

I didn't know if Alex would remember who Clay was. We'd never had any personal contact before. Not every boy in the organization knows exactly who or what I am, which has its advantages at times. It also had disadvantages at times. Like now. "Tell him it's Archie's boss," I said, which was close enough to the truth to do.

"Okay," she said, and in a minute a male voice came on, saying, "This is Alex."

"Clay here," I said. "Do you know a cop named Petry? Works the beat in your neighborhood, nights."

"Do I know you, buddy?" he asked me.

"Call Archie and find out," I said.

"I will. What'd you say the name was?"

"Clay. I'll call back in five minutes."

The five minutes dragged by, while I wished I'd just driven on down there, rather than call first. But it might have been a wasted trip, and I couldn't afford wasted trips.

When I called back, he said, "Who do you work for?"

"The same guy Archie does. Ed Ganolese. And you

can quit playing counterspy. Do you know a cop named Petry or don't you?"

"I know him."

"Can you get in touch with him?"

"Maybe."

"I want to talk to him. When can you set it up for?"

"Maybe Friday."

"Tonight. Right away."

"I'm not sure," he said.

"What did Archie tell you?" I asked him.

"How do I know you're Clay?"

"Crap," I said. "I'll be right down."

I slammed the phone down and headed for the door. Then I remembered Ella. I checked my watch and it was a quarter to two. I went back and called the Tambarin and left a message for Ella to wait for me at the bar, I'd be a little late. Then I left the apartment and headed downtown.

Chapter Twenty-One

La Sorina is one of a string of basement bars on that block of West 46th Street. When I went in, the place was full of girls, some sitting at the bar, some sitting at the booths along the right-hand wall. There was no one at all in the dining-room part of the place, to the back. A few guys were interspersed with the girls, pimps or hopefuls. Pick-ups aren't made here. This is just the spot where the girls get their phone calls.

Alex, behind the bar, was tall and fat and sour-looking. I squeezed between two of the girls, leaned against the bar, and waited for him to acknowledge my existence. It took a couple minutes, and then he walked over to stand in front of me and glower. "What's yours?" he asked me.

"Petry," I told him. "I'm the guy who called."

"Oh," he said. "You're Clay."

"That's right."

"I don't know why I should believe you," he said.

"Because I don't have time to fool around with you," I told him. "And because there's a place across the street that would like to take over your telephone business, and I'm in a position to say whether they get it or not."

He thought about it for a minute, and while he thought he drummed his fingers against the bar top.

He had thick fingers, huge hands. Finally, he turned to one of the girls and said something fast, in Spanish. She said something back, and then got off the stool and went out.

He looked at me again. "What are you drinking?" he asked me.

"Beer," I said.

He nodded and went away and came back with a beer.

"How long do I wait?" I asked him.

He shrugged. "Not long," he said. He drifted on down the bar and served his other customers.

The girl came back about five minutes later, reclaimed her place at the bar, and said something to Alex in Spanish. She didn't look at me at all. He nodded to her, came back over to me, and said, "Outside. Turn right, walk down to the parking lot. He's waiting for you there."

"Thanks," I said.

There were two possibilities, and as I walked toward the door I thought about the both of them. One, he believed me, and the cop was waiting for me down by the parking lot. Two, he didn't believe me, and a couple of people were waiting for me in the darkness between the front door and the steps up to the sidewalk.

I had to take a chance. I went out, moving fast, and didn't stop till I was up the three steps and standing on the pavement. Then I looked back. There hadn't been anyone waiting there.

I turned right and walked down toward the parking lot. A cop stood there, young and tall and slender, swinging his billy as though he'd just learned how. I stopped in front of him and said, "You're Alan Petry?"

"That's right," he said.

"You used to know a girl named Mavis St. Paul," I told him. "Back in your acting-class days."

"I did?"

"That's what Betty Benson said. Why, was she wrong?"

He shrugged. He had a college-boy face, square and bland and All-American. Beneath the hat, you could lay odds on there being a blond crew-cut. "I'm paid to walk," he told me. "Let's walk."

We walked, and I waited for him to decide to answer me. He did, finally, and said, "Mavis was just killed, wasn't she? Night before last."

"That's right," I said.

"What's your interest in her?"

"What's yours? Had you seen her recently?"

"I haven't seen or heard from Mavis since she shacked up with that bastard Grildquist."

"You don't like Grildquist?"

"He was old enough to be her father."

"But rich."

"He suckered her into thinking he was going to make a big Broadway star out of her."

"You didn't like it when she left you, is that it?"

"I might have killed her then," he said. "I wouldn't wait till now to do it."

"I hear you're married," I said.

"I am. Happily married. I've got two kids."

"Play around at all?"

"That's a hell of a question."

"What's the answer?"

"I'm not that kind of guy."

"You're the kind of guy who takes a little side money here and there," I reminded him.

He stopped and glared at me. "Who says so?"

"I do. Indirectly, I'm the guy who pays you."

"Me and everybody else," he said. "Let's say I don't take any money. So what? I report you to the sergeant, but you're paying him, too. So what do I gain? It's the system, and I work within it. That doesn't mean I play around with other women."

"Do you work Monday nights?"

"Sure."

"But you could walk off your beat for maybe half an hour without anybody noticing."

"I have to report every once in a while. Besides, I've got a partner."

"Where is he now?"

He jabbed a thumb in the direction we'd come from. "Back there in the diner, having coffee."

"So he doesn't see you all night long."

"I still have to report."

"You weren't working yesterday afternoon at four o'clock," I said.

"I was at school then."

"School?"

"I'm taking a couple of afternoon courses at Columbia. Working for a law degree."

"I could find out if you were really there yesterday."

"Sure you could. And they'd tell you yes."

"When was the last time you saw Mavis?"

"When she left me for Grildquist."

"And the last time you saw Betty Benson?"

"Her roommate? Same time, maybe a little later. I stayed around Paul Devon's classes a couple weeks more, then quit. That life wasn't for me."

I thought about guns. I'd been asking people if they had guns. Alan Petry had one, of course. It was strapped to his side. But I couldn't see myself asking him to let me look at it for a minute. Cops don't hand their guns to civilians.

We reached Ninth Avenue, turned around, and walked back toward Eighth again. Petry said, "You didn't tell me why you were so interested in Mavis."

"I'm following orders," I told him. That's always the simplest answer. A man following orders isn't expected to know why he's doing what he's doing. "I just do as I'm told, the same as everybody else."

"Sure," he said. "If you don't have anything else you want to ask me, maybe you ought to walk somewhere else. It probably doesn't look good, the two of us walking along together."

"All right," I said. "That was Columbia, you said?"

"That's right."

"Thanks for your time."

I walked faster, and he walked slower, and we weren't together any more. I headed down the block to the Mercedes, climbed in, and drove away, asking myself, what next, little man, what next?

Chapter Twenty-Two

I headed crosstown to the Tambarin, on 50th near Sixth. I left the Mercedes in a handy Kinney parking lot and walked down the block and into the bar half of the Tambarin.

She was at the bar, quietly ignoring the half-dozen guys who were trying to pick her up. She looked cool and beautiful, and her model's hatbox, in which she carts her costumes and make-up and so on, was on the floor beside her.

I stood in the doorway for a second, looking at her. I remembered Laura Marshall, and the double life Clancy has to lead because he's in the organization but he's married. Ella wasn't a Laura Marshall, not by a long shot. Could a guy who worked for the organization marry a girl like Ella and *not* have to live a double life?

Wrong subject, Clay, you're supposed to be thinking about the guy who killed Mavis St. Paul. And Betty Benson. And Billy-Billy Cantell.

I moved forward, pushing through the ever-hopeful stags at the bar, and touched Ella on the arm. She turned and smiled at me and said, "Oh, hi."

"Hi." I kissed her on the cheek, enjoying the envious looks from the stags, and said, "Let's go straight home. I'm in a mood for shoes-off drinking."

"Fine," she said.

We left the club and walked to the parking lot, both of us silent. Once in the car, she said, "How are you doing, Clay? With the murderer, I mean."

I filled her in, and she listened wide-eyed to the stories of the shot taken at me and the business in the subway station. "You could have been caught there," she said, when I was finished.

"I know. That occurred to me, too."

She thought about it for a minute, and then she said, "You say this man had an accent?"

"A phony. Muffled voice, accent, all phony."

"He didn't want you to hear his real voice."

"That's right."

"Why not?"

"Because—" I started, and then I stopped and just sat there for a minute, driving with half my mind and thinking about the fact that the guy had disguised his voice. Why? *Because he didn't want me to recognize him.*

Which meant I'd already talked to him before he ever got around to calling me. So scratch Alan Petry. And scratch Paul Devon.

And throw a great big spotlight on Ernest Tesselman.

"I'll be a son of a bitch," I said.

"That helps?" she asked me.

"That helps," I told her. I grinned at her. "Come on over here, genius," I said, "and let me drive one-handed for a while."

She came on over and I drove one-handed, and I

put the Mercedes away for the night. The Puerto Rican kid didn't say anything to me about the job, probably because he wasn't sure the girl I was with could be trusted. I winked at him to let him know I hadn't forgotten him, and he grinned at me.

It seemed as though the phone was always ringing when I walked into that apartment lately. Or the cops were waiting for me, one or the other. This time it was the phone, and when I picked up the receiver, Archie Freihofer oozed into my ear and snuggled. "I've been trying to reach you, baby," he cooed.

"I just got home. What's the good word?"

"None, baby. I'm sorry. Johnny Ricardo's the only steady customer on this list you gave me, and he wasn't with any of my girls at either time you're interested in. The others are all strangers."

"That's too bad," I said.

"Sorry, sweetie."

"Sure, Archie. Thanks for trying."

"Any time."

I hung up, took a step toward the beer in the refrigerator, and the phone rang again. Ella smiled at me from across the room. "You're a popular man," she said.

"I wanted a beer."

"I'll get it. You talk to your public."

This time it was Junky Stein. "I found out where Paul Devon was at four o'clock yesterday afternoon," he said.

"Good boy. Where?"

"In class, acting class. With twelve students."

"He didn't duck out for a few minutes?"

"He was directing two of the kids in a scene, the way I hear it. There every minute."

"Well, so there you are. Thanks, Junky."

"I haven't heard from Billy-Billy at all," he said.

"I have," I told him. "I'm sorry, Junky. He's dead."

"Billy-Billy? Clay, you promised me—"

"It wasn't us, Junky. I'm looking for the guy. It's the same one killed the two women."

"Level, Clay?"

"Level, Junky."

"I hope you find him, Clay. Billy-Billy never hurt anybody."

After that call, I dragged out my notebook again, and looked at the names I hadn't crossed out yet. Three of them. Johnny Ricardo. Ernest Tesselman. The husband. Ricardo was a dark horse, as far as I was concerned. If he turned out to be the guy I was after, I would be damn surprised.

That left Tesselman and the husband. Tesselman was a phony, faking affection for a girl who'd been nothing more to him than steady tail. That didn't necessarily make him a killer, but it did make him a bit more likely a suspect than if he'd played it straight. I'd have to go talk to him again tomorrow, and I'd have to find some way to check his movements at the time of the murders. And the husband. I liked him for the job, more and more. He and Tesselman, as far as I was concerned, were neck and neck in the Cutie Sweepstakes. It didn't make a hell of a lot of sense for him to wait five years to kill Mavis, but maybe it would when I found out just who he was. He was my favorite, with Tesselman, principally because I knew so little about him.

"Your beer, Clay," said Ella.

I looked up, and she was standing in front of me, holding out the glass. "I didn't hear you come back," I said. "Thanks."

"You want to think for a while, don't you?"

"I'm down to three people," I told her. "That's two too many."

"I won't disturb you."

But she did. She had to. She sat very quietly over on the other side of the room, sipping a beer, and just being there she distracted me. I had to come to a decision about her, and until I did, I was going to have trouble thinking about anything else, particularly in the same room with her.

We sat in silence for a while, and then I said, "Ella, what do you think about me? What do you think about the business I'm in?"

She looked over at me, surprised. "Why, Clay?"

"I want to know, that's all. What you think of me, and what you think of the business."

"I like you," she said. "I don't like your business. You made it plain this afternoon that you're in the business to stay, no matter what." She shrugged.

"Do you understand why?" I asked her.

"No, not really," she said. "I understand you feel loyalty to Ed Ganolese, you feel you owe him something—"

"My freedom," I said. "I'd be in jail now if it weren't for him."

"Do you call your life freedom?" she asked me.

"Of course. I'm damn near my own boss. I work my own hours, I make a good living, most of the time things are calm and quiet and peaceful. Every once in a while the law gets upset, but it blows over and things are peaceful again."

"You don't have any feelings about the morality of what you're doing?"

"As a cop told me tonight," I said, "I work within the system. Guys like Ed Ganolese, and the organizations they control, exist only because the average citizen *wants* them to exist. The average citizen *wants* an organization that can supply a nice, reliable whore when he's in the mood. The average citizen *wants* an organization that runs after-hours drinking places for the nights when Average Citizen doesn't feel like going home at closing time. The average citizen likes a union that's a little crooked, because he knows some of the gravy's going to seep down to him. The average citizen even likes to know there's some place where he can pick up some marijuana if he feels like being wild and Bohemian for a while. And with the number of drug addicts in this country numbering over a hundred thousand, I'm talking about the average citizen. The average citizen also likes to gamble, to buy his imported whiskey cheap, and to read in the papers about desperate gangsters. The average citizen votes for crooked politicians and *knows* they're crooked politicians when he votes for them. But maybe he'll get something off his property assessment, or he'll be able to pick up a little graft. At the very least, he'll get his kicks by knowing somebody else is picking up some graft."

"That's all rationalization, Clay, and you know it," she said.

"It isn't rationalization, it's the truth. It's the way the system works and the reason for the system's existence, and I work within the system." I got to my feet and paced back and forth, warming to my subject. It was a subject I'd thought about often during the last nine years. "Simple economics shows it's the way the system works," I said. "Look, no business can survive if it doesn't get support from the consumer, right?"

"Clay, this isn't a *business*."

"But it is. We don't rob banks, for God's sake. We run a business. We have items for sale or for rent, and the goddam general public buys. Girls or drugs or higher wages or whatever it is, we give something for the money we get. We're a business, and we wouldn't last a minute if we weren't supported by our goddam buying public."

"There are legal businesses, Clay."

"Sure there are. And they operate the same way we do. They fight and claw for the customer's dollar. They do their damnedest to get rid of the competition. They try to produce something the consumer is going to buy. Within their organization, if somebody isn't producing, they fire him. And you know when they do most of their firing? At Christmastime, if you want to talk about morality. They fire at Christmastime, because January is a bad month for business. When we fire somebody, we do it permanently, that's the only difference. We do it permanently because we can't afford to have people outside the organization who know too much about organization matters. And don't tell me the big corporations don't wish they could fire permanently, too, rather than see their ex-employees going over to the competition to spread the word on what Amalgamated Incorporated is planning to do next year."

"Clay, haven't you repaid your debt to Ed Ganolese?"

"Crap," I said. "I'm not in this business purely and simply out of a sense of duty. There's more to it than that."

"The thing is," she said, "you like the business. And you like the feeling of power the business gives you. You like being a big-shot syndicate man."

"Of course I do. Who ever said I didn't?"

"You've been talking around it ever since I met you, Clay."

"All right," I said. I sat down beside her again. "I like the job, all right? That's me, the big bad nasty man who works for the big bad crooks and likes it."

"You don't have to talk to me about it if you don't want to," she said.

"Ella, why did you move in with me? I met you, I took you out a couple of times, I said move in with me, and you said all right. Why?"

"Because I liked you. Why else?"

"You didn't know me as well then as you do now."

"I knew what business you were in."

"The hell you did. It was all mysterious and secretive, and you didn't know a thing about it. And you didn't want to know a thing about it. Every time business came up, you faded out of sight, so you wouldn't have to know about it."

"I thought you wanted me to do that."

"I did. Now, I don't. Now, I want you to know as much about me as you can."

"Why?"

"Because I want to know if you still like me."

"I'm sitting here, aren't I?"

"For how long?"

She didn't answer for a long minute. She looked away from me and sipped at her drink and lit a cigarette, and I waited for her to say something. Finally, she said, "If you're working up to a proposal, you're taking the strangest method I ever heard of."

"Clancy Marshall's married," I said. "His wife makes believe Clancy's a lawyer like any other lawyer. He doesn't talk about his work at home, he has to keep up a pretty little fiction with his wife's friends, he has to make believe he's somebody else every minute he's with her. Ed Ganolese is married, too. He's got a daughter at some exclusive girls' college up in New England. He has to play a part at home, too. I don't want a marriage like that. I want a woman to marry *me*, not some figment of her imagination that I'm supposed to conform to."

"You want a woman who would marry a syndicate gangster," she said.

"Crap. I want a woman who will marry *me*."

"Isn't that the same thing?"

"I don't know, maybe it is."

"Would you have any respect for a woman who would marry a syndicate gangster?"

"Who the hell is talking about respect?"

"I am," she said. "Clay, when I moved in here, you played that pretty little fiction you were talking about. You didn't object when I avoided any mention of your work. But now, for the last couple of days, you've been showing me more and more of what your life is like. And I keep wondering, what can he think of a woman who will stay with him even after he shows her what he does for a living? How can he think I'm anything but a common whore?"

"Would I propose to a common whore, you clown? Don't be silly."

"Don't syndicate gangsters always marry common whores?"

"No. That's out of stories."

"I don't know, Clay," she said. "Let me think about it. I don't want to give you an answer yet."

"Do you want to stay here while you think about it?"

"Yes," she said. "But—I think we should just go right to sleep tonight."

"Oh."

She reached out and took my hand. "Don't read an answer into that, Clay," she said. "It's just that I've got this to think about, and I don't feel like—like anything else."

"All right," I said.

She got to her feet. "I'm going to bed now," she said. "I'm exhausted. Are you coming?"

"Not yet. I'll be along after a while."

"Clay—" She stopped and shrugged her shoulders. "We'll talk tomorrow."

"Sure," I said.

She kissed me, a brief emotionless kiss, and then she stepped away from me again. "You look like a worried little boy," she said.

"I am a worried little boy."

"Playing cops and robbers."

"Sure."

I watched her go, and I spent a while thinking about her. I didn't know whether she'd stay or not, and I wasn't even sure whether I *wanted* her to stay or not. All I knew was that she was the first girl in nine years who had made me wonder about things like this. She was the first girl in nine years who made me want to justify myself.

Face it, Clay. She was the first girl in nine years to make me think of quitting Ed Ganolese.

Chapter Twenty-Three

When I woke up, a little after noon, Ella wasn't in the apartment. She'd left a note, on the kitchen table. Just three words: "I'll be back."

So she hadn't made her decision yet, and she didn't want to talk to me until she'd made it. In the meantime, I could just sweat it out, and try to make my own decision. I had to decide if it would be possible to be married to Ella and still work for Ed Ganolese. If that wasn't possible, I had to choose between them.

Last night, we'd come close to the heart of the thing. Ella was right, I *did* like working for Ed Ganolese. I liked everything about it. I liked the feeling of being Ed Ganolese's strong right arm. I was high enough in the organization so that no one in the world but Ed Ganolese could give me orders. At the same time, I wasn't in a position of final authority, where the power-hungry boys would like to rush me to the graveyard so they could take over. It was a safe and strong position, one of the safest and strongest in the world, and I liked having it.

And I liked the work. I liked being the guy who carries the orders to the team, who whips the kiddies back in line when they do wrong, who kisses them goodbye when they have to be taken off the payroll.

I don't mean I enjoy killing, don't get me wrong.

I'm called on for something like that very rarely—most of the time, my job is simply to assign the few killings we do have to make to professional triggermen affiliated with the organization—and when I have to do it myself, I turn emotion off completely until it's over with. Killing is an occasional business necessity with the organization, and I believe in keeping it on a business level. I neither hate nor pity. My attitude is the same as any personnel manager who has to fire an unneeded or annoying employee.

The professional triggermen do enjoy killing, though most of them won't admit it. But why else get into that line of work? That's why triggermen don't last very long. They're emotional, and whenever you mix business with emotion, you're in for trouble.

I remember talking to one of them one time, a triggerman who *would* admit he enjoyed his job. "Sure I like killing," he told me. "Who doesn't? Nobody's ever come back from a war claiming they didn't like it when they killed. The only thing that mars the pleasure of killing in a war is the fact that the other guys are shooting back. That doesn't happen with me, so I can enjoy a killing without worrying about it happening to me."

We spent one long afternoon together, that guy and I, drinking beer in a joint on Eighth Avenue, and he kept hitting the same theme over and over again. "I enjoy killing," he said, "exactly the same way that everybody else enjoys killing. Look, here I am, let's say, I'm holding a gun, and there's this guy in front of me, standing there, someone I never met in my life before but somebody wants him dead and I got the job. Okay?

Okay. I squeeze the trigger, see, and the gun in my hand jumps like a live thing, roaring, and the guy standing in front of me crumples like old tissue paper. I enjoy that, I enjoy the feeling of the gun in my hand, I enjoy the sight of some guy crumpling up and falling to the ground."

I asked him why he could enjoy a thing like that, and he told me. "Because it isn't happening to me," he said. "Death is always interesting, Clay, it's always a kick. Ask the crowd standing around an automobile accident, or the crowd waiting on the sidewalk for the guy on the ledge to fall or jump, or the crowd at a public execution. They're enjoying themselves, Clay, those people, the same way I enjoy myself when I pull the trigger and the guy falls down dead. They're enjoying themselves because death is near and it isn't their own death. That's the exact same way I enjoy doing a killing. Most people are afraid to do a killing themselves, afraid of the law or afraid of reprisals or something like that. But I'm not afraid. I let the enjoyment come through, the relief and the kick that I'm still alive, I'm still breathing. *He's* dead, but I'm still alive."

It's an easy thing to take your own private sickness and claim everybody else has it too, so it really isn't a sickness after all. And who could tell this guy, if he were still alive—the cops got him, finally, when he was enjoying himself so much after one job he couldn't bring himself to leave the body—that he's wrong, that the sickness is real, and almost exclusively his own?

A guy who's never killed can't say whether killing is enjoyable or not. I've killed, so I can refute that madman.

I've never killed a man I hated. I've never killed a man who was doing any good for society in being alive. I've never killed a man for personal reasons of any kind.

I've killed. Only a few times, but I have killed, and I've never enjoyed it. It's been strictly business, strictly a job I'm supposed to do. And I know if I let any emotion come out at all, it wouldn't be enjoyment, it would be pity. And then I wouldn't be able to do it.

What I *do* enjoy is the reputation I've got. Ed knows all he has to do is point a finger and say, "Clay, that guy has to stop breathing, don't farm it out," and he knows the guy will stop breathing, and I won't farm it out to one of the professional triggermen, and I won't do a sloppy job of it. The law has never come near us for any killing I've done personally.

That's part of the reputation. Dependability, no matter what. I enjoy knowing I've got that reputation, and I enjoy knowing I deserve it. The other part is that the people in the organization who know me, or know of me, know I'm the best damn watchdog Ed Ganolese has ever had. They know I can't be bought, they know I can't be scared, they know I can't be outfoxed. They know I can turn emotion off, and they know no man has ever been trapped except through his emotions.

A guy like that triggerman, the one who'd admit that he got a kick out of killing somebody, he worries me and he makes me uneasy. A guy like that isn't reliable, isn't trustworthy. Ed could never put a guy who thought like that in my job. He needs somebody like me, who can kill when he has to, but who doesn't get to like the taste of blood.

I thought about that, and I wondered if it would ever be possible to explain it all to Ella. How to explain to her that I kill *only* in cold blood, but that that doesn't make me cold-blooded? That I am emotionless only when emotion is dangerous, and that I am as emotional as the next man under normal circumstances.

I didn't think I could explain it at all, not to her and not to anybody else. I doubted I could explain anything about my relationship with the organization, and how it is possible for me to do all the things required of me by the organization, and still remain myself.

Possible? No, that wasn't the word. Necessary was the word. I couldn't explain to her how or why it was necessary for me to do everything required of me by the organization, and still remain myself. I couldn't explain to her that any man with a vocation absolutely needs to be needed in that vocation, and that my vocation was to be Ed Ganolese's good right hand.

Which brought me right back to the original question. Could I be married to Ella and still be working for Ed Ganolese at the same time?

I had an unhappy feeling the answer to that question was no. Which in turn raised the second question. Which did I want more, my current life and job, or Ella?

That one I couldn't answer at all.

While I brooded about it, I made myself some breakfast and then wandered around the apartment for a while, at loose ends. Finally, I pushed the problem into the back of my mind, picked up my notebook, settled myself in the living room, and went back to the other problem, namely, who killed Mavis St. Paul et al., and why?

It occurred to me that it was just barely possible that the killer wasn't on my list at all. But who else was there? I'd asked around, I'd poked and pried, but no more names had cropped up. He *had* to be here, he had to be one of the three names left.

And if the list kept getting smaller, until it reached zero?

I'd worry about that when it happened.

Of my two favorites, Ernest Tesselman and the husband, Tesselman was the only one I could do anything about at the moment. I had to wait on the husband until I heard from East St. Louis.

It seemed like time to have another little chat with Ernest Tesselman. I called Ed, told him what I wanted to do, and got Tesselman's home phone number from him. Then I called Tesselman, told him who I was, and said I wanted to have another little chat with him.

"Are the police still bothering you?" he asked me.

"No," I said. "They've eased off. I appreciate that, Mr. Tesselman."

"Then what do you want to talk about?"

"I'd rather tell you in person, sir."

"Not here," he said. "I'll be at my office at four o'clock." He gave me the address, on Fifth Avenue just south of Central Park, and I told him I'd be there at four.

That left me with three hours, and nothing to do. So I did nothing. I brooded about Ella, and I brooded about the cutie, and around two-thirty the phone rang.

I hurried to answer it, hoping it was the call from East St. Louis, but it was only Clancy Marshall, spouting doom and gloom again. "Clay," he said. "Can't you talk some sense into Ed?"

"What's wrong now?"

"What do you think is wrong? This cops-and-robbers game you're playing. Clay, I don't know whether Ed has told you this or not, but the organization is going to hell while you two play around in matters that don't concern us at all. I was just talking to Starkweather, our accountant, and this thing is costing us money, more money than we can afford."

"What do you expect me to do?"

"Talk to Ed. He won't listen to me."

"He won't listen to me either, Clancy. He wants the guy who started this mess."

"And then what? Clay, look at it realistically. The police have Billy-Billy Cantell, so the case is closed. We can't turn this guy over to the law."

"I don't think Ed plans to turn him over to the law."

"What else? Kill him?"

"I think that's what he has in mind, yes."

"Fine. Then we've got the law upset all over again. This isn't like killing some little punk in the organization, Clay. You're going to be killing somebody who's a solid citizen as far as the law is concerned. So we'll have another investigation on our hands."

"Maybe not. We can probably cover it."

"Maybe. Probably. We don't stay in business with maybes and probablys, Clay."

"Clancy, tell me something. Is Ed sore at you for harping on this?"

"He won't even listen to me any more. I call his place and that Neanderthal bodyguard of his just hangs up on me."

"So you want me to talk to him. Clancy, if I talked to him it wouldn't do any good. He'd just be sore at me, too. If he won't take advice from his lawyer, he won't take it from me."

"We can't keep fooling around this way, Clay."

"Maybe it won't last much longer."

"You're getting close to him?"

"I think so."

"Well, that's some consolation. I say we should forget the whole thing, but I'll be just as happy to see it finished with once and for all."

"Don't take your job so seriously, Clancy."

"I'm paid to take it seriously," he said.

After that, I brooded about one thing and another for a while longer, and a little after three Ella came home. I started to say something to her, but she interrupted me, saying, "Not yet, Clay. I don't want to talk about it yet. Have you had any lunch?"

"No," I said.

So we had some lunch, and we didn't talk about it. But since that was all either of us was thinking about, we didn't talk about anything else either. It was a long and silent lunch.

Chapter Twenty-Four

Tesselman's office suite was on the fourteenth floor, and the frosted glass window showed gold lettering reading "Ernest Tesselman, Attorney-at-Law." But Ernest Tesselman hadn't been a practicing attorney, in the normal sense of the phrase, in years.

He was the only one present in the suite, by which I mean there was no secretary. The butler-bouncer was present, dressed in civvies and now converted to bodyguard, but bodyguards don't count among those present.

The atmosphere was somewhat chillier at this meeting than it had been the first time. The bodyguard, whom I still thought of as Tux even though he was in mufti now, was waiting for me in the outer office, and he insisted on frisking me before letting me in to see his boss. His search was thorough, but I wasn't wearing any armament of any kind, so he grudgingly held the door open for me, and I walked on into Ernest Tesselman's sanctum sanctorum.

Tesselman was formally dressed this time, in a somewhat old-fashioned blue-gray suit, complete with vest and watch chain. The desk he sat behind was as huge and as empty as the desk in his study at home. He motioned me into the leather chair opposite him, and Tux stood watchfully in a corner behind his boss.

"I'll begin," I said, "by filling you in on events since I last talked to you."

He nodded, silent, waiting for me to get to the point. His eyes were cold and wary, not trusting me.

"Betty Benson was killed," I said, "shortly after I talked with you."

"I know," he said. "I read about it in the newspaper. The police had some idea you did it."

"I'd been there, before the murderer. At any rate, Billy-Billy Cantell, the one they wanted for the killing of Miss St. Paul, is also dead, and the police have the body. So the case is closed, as far as they're concerned."

"As far as they're concerned?"

"Ed Ganolese isn't satisfied. We've had a lot of trouble and a lot of expense because of this. Ed wants to even the score."

"So you're still looking."

"That's right, I am."

"Why come to me? I told you everything I knew the last time we talked."

"I'm afraid you were lying to me, Mr. Tesselman."

He glanced over at Tux, who hadn't moved, and then looked back at me. "That's a rude thing to say. Also inaccurate."

"I said I'd talked to Betty Benson before she was killed. You and she differed on a couple of points."

"Such as?"

"You told Mavis, and you also told me, that you were

planning on helping her get started in musical comedy."

"That's right."

"Miss Benson told me Mavis couldn't carry a tune, couldn't sing a note."

"She was merely untrained. I was paying for singing lessons."

"You also told Mavis, she says, that you were planning to marry her."

"I had asked her to marry me, that's right."

"Yet you tried to seduce Miss Benson."

"Did she tell you that? She's a filthy little liar."

"Why? Why should she lie about it?"

"Having known the girl only slightly, I couldn't begin to guess what her motives were."

"You tried to give me the impression you'd been in love with Mavis St. Paul, that her death affected you deeply."

"And?"

"I'm afraid it became apparent, after a while, that you cared more for that pregnant fish of yours than you did for Mavis."

"Your rudeness knows no bounds, I see," he said. "Nor does your bad taste. Aside from the untruth of your suggestions and statements, I'd like to know what business you have making them. What are you doing here?"

"Hadn't it occurred to you that you were a logical suspect?"

"Suspect? You think I killed Mavis?"

"No, sir. Nor do I think you didn't. But I do think there's a possibility that you killed her. And there are

ome contradictions in your attitude toward her. I'm
ere to try to straighten out those contradictions."

"The last time you visited me," he said coldly, "I tried
o be reasonable. I don't feel like being reasonable this
me. You come here and suggest I murdered that poor
irl, suggest that my attitude toward her was hypocrit-
al, that I lied to you before. I see no purpose in being
easonable."

"As you wish."

He glared at me and gnawed on his lower lip. "I could
reak you," he said at last. "I could break Ed Ganolese."

"I don't know anything about that," I said.

"You know that I can influence the Police Depart-
ent to make life difficult for you and your employer.
did it once. Why shouldn't I do it now?"

"Because you were in love with Mavis St. Paul," I
aid, "and you quite naturally want to help us find the
an who killed her."

"I see. And if I don't cooperate, that means I'm a
ypocrite. You'll have things your own way, won't you?"

"No, sir. I can only ask. We'll have things your way."

"You're glib," he said. He sat back, frowning, and
tudied the empty expanse of his desktop. Tux stood
olidly in the corner, watching a point in mid-air some-
here between his boss and myself. I waited, sitting
nse in my chair, wanting a cigarette but knowing I
houldn't move until Tesselman had thought it out and
ome to a decision.

When he spoke again, he did so without moving,
ithout turning his gaze away from the desktop. "I was
nd of Mavis," he said. "She wanted to marry me. I

never fooled myself that she loved me. I'm an old man
she was a young woman. She wanted to marry me because she liked me, she could tolerate living with me
and she would have fine prospects of being a wealthy
widow in just a few years. I understood that. I also
understood that her terms were better than I could
expect to find from any other woman of her age. Mavis
was interested in my money, but she was also interested in me. I'm convinced of that. She would not live
with a man simply because he was rich. If he was rich
and she could like him, then she would live with him."

He looked up at me then, his eyes hard beneath
frowning brows. "This is painful for me to talk about,"
he said. "When Mavis died, I was shocked. She was, if
you prefer, a valued possession. I didn't love her, but I
was fond of her, and I was aware that she was the last
woman who could possibly be interested in me. I did
everything I could think of to keep that interest alive.
Of course she couldn't sing, but she didn't know that.
I promised to help her make a name for herself in
musical comedy. I promised her anything she wanted
to keep that interest alive. When she spoke of marriage, I promised her that, too. Even knowing our
marriage would be, on her part, one long deathwatch,
I promised to marry her. She was my last chance."

He got suddenly to his feet, turned away from me,
and stumped over to stare out the window at Fifth
Avenue. "I'm a proud man," he said, his back to me. "I
don't like to admit the weakness of my relationship
with Mavis. When I heard she was dead, she'd been
murdered, I was shocked and I was outraged. A pos-

ession of mine, something of value to me, had been destroyed. I talked to a friend on the Police Department, told him I wanted a fast arrest and a fast conviction. I was vindictive, justifiably so. But later on, I saw the whole thing in a different light. I was an old man who had made a fool of himself over a young woman. When you came to talk to me, I didn't want you to know that. I didn't want anyone to know what a fool and what a weakling I had been. I have always prided myself on my strength."

The room was silent again as he stared out the window. Then he turned and looked at me. "That's what you wanted to know," he said. "Now you can leave. Find the man who killed Mavis, if you want. I don't care. One gets over the loss of a possession, no matter how valuable it once seemed."

"Mr. Tesselman—"

"I think I see you pitying me," he said. "The last thing in the world I want is your cheap pity. I've never in my life needed pity, and I don't need pity now."

"Mr. Tesselman," I said again, but he turned his back once more and looked out the window.

Tux took a step toward me. "It's time to leave, buddy," he said.

I left.

Chapter Twenty-Five

I knew Ella would still be at the apartment, and I didn't want to go home and sit around beneath that heavy silence again. It was now nearly four-thirty, and she would be leaving for work at seven o'clock, so I had two and a half hours to kill.

I spent the time in a bar half a block from Ernest Tesselman's office, and I spent my time thinking about the Mavis St. Paul killing, and refusing to think about Ella.

Sitting in the booth, a Scotch and water on the table in front of me, I opened the notebook and looked at the three names left there. I had now talked to Ernest Tesselman again, and I was convinced that this time he'd told me the truth. Whether he had told me all the truth or not was another question. I was sure his relationship with Mavis St. Paul was just as he had described it. But what if Mavis had backed out at the last minute? What if she had suddenly decided it wasn't worth it, marrying an old geezer like Ernest Tesselman? As Tesselman had said, Mavis was his last chance. What if she'd taken that chance away from him? There was a lot of rage boiling deep within that old man. I'd seen glimpses of it. If Mavis had turned him down, if she'd told him she was leaving him, he might have grown just furious enough to grab a knife and stab her to death. Then, knowing he was a natural suspect, he hurried out of the apartment, found someone to take his place as suspect number one, and went home prepared to be grief-stricken when he got the news.

And then it hit me. Why it hadn't before I don't know, but all at once I realized it couldn't have happened that way. Mavis St. Paul was killed in an apartment on East 63rd Street. Junky Stein had seen Billy-Billy passed out in an alleyway beside a movie theater, earlier that night, on East 6th Street, fifty-seven blocks away. Aside from the fact that it would have taken the better part of an hour to make the round trip, there was no necessity for the killer to go all the way to 6th Street to find a passed-out bum.

Up until now, I'd been figuring the case from the viewpoint that Billy-Billy had been chosen by accident, but it didn't make sense that way. The cutie hadn't gone out looking for any old stumblebum, he'd gone out looking for Billy-Billy Cantell.

Not only that, he'd gone out to get Billy-Billy *first*, before he killed Mavis St. Paul. He found Billy-Billy, stuffed him into the car, drove up to Mavis's place, brought Billy-Billy upstairs, carried him into the apartment, dumped him on the sofa, knifed Mavis, and left. Of course that was the way it had happened. Not two trips to Mavis's apartment, only one trip. Our boy planned too carefully to risk returning to the apartment after Mavis was dead.

Which left Ernest Tesselman out. I could see Tesselman, enraged, suddenly murdering Mavis St. Paul, and then trying to figure out some way to get himself off the hook. But I couldn't see him *planning* to murder Mavis. He had no reason to kill her that would hold up after calm and careful reflection. He might kill her in white-hot anger, but he wouldn't be killing her while calm.

I could cross his name off the list, leaving only Johnny Ricardo and the husband. I would have crossed Johnny Ricardo's name off, too, but I didn't want to limit myself to one suspect until I found out a hell of a lot more about the husband than I knew right now.

I sat around in the bar, thinking about one thing and another until almost seven-thirty, and then I went home. I had twenty-five blocks to go, and it was still hot out, though not as oppressively muggy as it had been the last few days, but I decided to walk. I was in no hurry to be alone in the apartment. Out here on the street, I could think about the heat and the taxicabs and the fairies lined up along Central Park West, looking hopefully with gray-ringed round eyes at all the men hurrying by. I could think about Mavis St. Paul and Ernest Tesselman and the husband. I could think about Ed Ganolese and Billy-Billy Cantell and half a million other things.

In the apartment, I would only be able to think of Ella.

I arrived at my building finally, went up in the elevator, and walked into the apartment just as the phone started ringing. I shut the door and hurried across the room to pick up the receiver.

The voice said, "Clay? This is Tex."

"Who?"

"You know. From East St. Louis."

"Oh," I said. "Oh, yeah. Tex."

"I've been trying to call since four-thirty," he said. "There wasn't anybody home."

Which meant Ella had gone out again. To avoid me? "I just walked in the front door this minute," I said. "Did you get the information I wanted?"

"Sure. She married one of the Air Force officers out at the air base." And he told me the name of the killer.

I thanked him, and I hung up, and then I just sat and stared at the wall for a while. Because now I knew what the connection was between Billy-Billy Cantell and the guy who had killed Mavis St. Paul.

Because Mavis St. Paul had been married to First Lieutenant Michael Cantell.

Chapter Twenty-Six

I spent a while just sitting there in my living room, a
it gradually grew dark outside the windows, and i
gradually grew light inside my mind. I let the thought
come to me, and piece by piece the whole thing came
together.

I remembered the fact I'd noticed but hadn't made
anything of at the time, the fact that Billy-Billy Cantel
had gone into that subway station alive and had been
murdered right there. Which could only mean he'c
gone down there with somebody he knew and trusted
Michael Cantell. Good old Mike.

And now I knew where Billy-Billy had gone afte
he'd run away from my place, way back at the beginning of this mess. He'd gone off to see good old Mike

I wondered what the relationship was. Brothers
Cousins? Not that it really mattered. The point was tha
the relationship was there, and Billy-Billy had placed
his trust in that relationship, and Michael Cantell, the
bastard, had killed him.

Good old Mike had set him up in the first place
come to think of it. And now I saw that scene a lot more
clearly, too. Billy-Billy is full of heroin, snoozing awa
in that alley beside the theater. Good old Mike (cousin
brother?) comes along and says, "Hop in, Billy-Billy
and we'll go for a little ride." Billy-Billy hops in, but he

doesn't remember it later on. Maybe he doesn't even recognize Mike when it happens. I remembered how long it had taken Junky Stein to recognize me.

All right, that was the way it happened. Now the question was: Why did Michael Cantell do it that way? Why does he set his own relative up, of all people, to take the rap for his killing?

And there was an answer for that one, too. Because he wanted to get rid of Billy-Billy.

Then why didn't he just stick the same knife into Billy-Billy, and forget it?

There was a possible reason for that. Let's say Michael Cantell came to New York when he deserted Mavis St. Paul. Let's say he's made good in the last five years, he's done well for himself. Now, add Billy-Billy. A relative, most likely a brother. And he's a bum. He's got a monkey on his back bigger than King Kong. He's a disgrace to the family. He's an annoyance. Not big enough an annoyance to kill, since a relative would be a natural suspect, but big enough to keep Michael Cantell irritated. Big enough an annoyance so that, when our boy Mike Cantell does decide somebody has to get killed, Billy-Billy is his natural choice for the patsy. He kills two birds with one knife. He gets rid of Mavis, the one he'd decided to kill, and at the same time he gets rid of Billy-Billy, that family annoyance. Chop. Chop. All problems solved.

That was half of his motive. The other half concerned Mavis. For all I'd been able to find out, he and Mavis hadn't seen each other for five years. She didn't even know he was in New York. Why should he wait five years to kill her? What had happened recently, what had changed recently, that suddenly made it necessary for him to kill her?

And then I remembered something Betty Benson had told me. Mavis had seen a lawyer about getting a divorce. A divorce, that was the change. For some reason, Mavis's starting divorce proceedings had forced the murder.

How?

Maybe he was married again. Maybe he was rich now, and Mavis was about to put the screws to him. She'd apparently been that type of girl.

Yes, but they still had to meet somehow, they still had to get together after a five-year separation.

And then I remembered something else Betty Benson had told me. Something she had said that had seemed so slight at the time that I hadn't even bothered to copy it down in my notebook. Something that she alone, out of all the people in New York, was likely to know. The thing that had forced Michael Cantell to kill her.

And then I knew who Michael Cantell was today. I knew the face of the murderer.

I reached out to the phone and called Ed Ganolese. When he came on the line, I said, "I've got him, Ed. I've got the cutie."

"Are you sure? Are you one hundred percent positive?"

"I'm one thousand percent positive, Ed. I've got the goods on him. Call a meeting of the board, will you? In Clancy's office at"—I looked at my watch, and it was eight-thirty—"at nine-thirty. That'll give everybody time to get there."

"Where is he, Clay? Where is the bastard?"

"Wait a second, now," I said. "You don't want to go off half-cocked. And you don't want me to go off half-cocked, either. I'll go over the whole thing with you, every step of the way. That's why I want a meeting of the board. I want you people to double-check my thinking on this thing and tell me whether I'm right or wrong."

"You've got it, though. You're sure of that."

"I've got it, Ed. I've got this guy pinned to the wall like a butterfly."

"Okay. Nine-thirty, at Clancy's office."

"Right. And bring Joe Pistol along. He might be interested."

"I'll have to bring him along. This thing has been lousing things up all over the place. Joe isn't very happy about it, and he's clinging to me like a leech."

"He'll be happy soon," I said. "And so will you."

Chapter Twenty-Seven

Clancy opened the office door for me when I knocked. He grinned that grin of his and said, "I hear you're the boy genius of the hour."

"I'm the boy genius of the week," I told him.

"You mean this is really finished now?"

"It's really finished."

We walked on through to the inner office. Ed and Tony and Joe Pistol hadn't shown up yet. Starkweather, the accountant, was there, sitting off in a corner and looking uncomfortable and out of place. "How come you're here?" I asked him.

"I called him and asked him to come over," Clancy told me. "Ed should know what's been happening this week. Fred here can fill him in."

"That can happen second," I said.

Starkweather bobbed his balding accountant's head. "Certainly," he said. "First things first."

"Sure." I went over and looked out the window. Far below me was the canyon of the street, cabs swimming back and forth down there like the tropical fish Ernest Tesselman kept. I looked around the office and I saw the framed photograph of Clancy's wife, standing on the desk. Clancy was married. Ed Ganolese was married. Even fussy little Starkweather over there was married. Why shouldn't I get married?

While I was struggling to keep from thinking about that, Ed came in, followed by Tony and Joe Pistol. Everybody sat down, and Ed said, "Okay, Clay. Let's hear it."

I told him first about the phone call from East St. Louis, and what the relationship between Michael Cantell and Billy-Billy Cantell had to mean. And what the relationship between Michael Cantell and Mavis St. Paul had to mean. And then I said, "Betty Benson had the key all along. She told it to me, but I didn't notice. The thing was, what caused the killing in the first place was the fact that Mavis St. Paul went to see a lawyer about a divorce. For a while, I figured the fact that Mavis wanted a divorce had somehow or other forced the killing. But then I remembered what it was Betty Benson had told me. Mavis had married somebody from the air base out near her home town. She'd been working at the air base, and that's where she met him. And she'd been working in the legal office."

I grinned at them all. "See it? She married a lawyer. And when she decided to get herself a divorce, what lawyer did she go to see? Out of all the lawyers in New York, she picked her own husband. Of course, he'd changed his name in the meantime, so she didn't realize who he was until she walked into his office. But when she saw the kind of office he had, when she saw the obvious signs that Mike Cantell was now making lots of money, all of a sudden she didn't want a divorce at all. And then she found out he'd gone and gotten himself married again. For a girl like Mavis, that meant only one thing. She could get bigger alimony for not divorcing him than she could if she went ahead and got the divorce as planned. In less polite circles, that kind of alimony is called blackmail."

In the silence, I looked over at Clancy. "Where'd she get your name, Mike?" I asked him. "From Ernest Tesselman? Did he mention you once or twice, in connection with Ed Ganolese? Or did she just pull the old coincidence bit?"

Clancy's smile looked like something made of melting wax. "I don't get you, Clay," he said, but his voice broke twice while he was saying it.

"You don't get me, Mike," I told him. "But I get you. I get you cold."

Ed was glaring at Clancy. "Is this on the level?" he demanded.

Clancy said, "Of course not, Ed. It's the most ridiculous thing I ever heard of." The way he said it, the greenest girl scout in the country could have seen he was lying.

"Clancy Marshall," I said. "You couldn't get away from that amateur stunt of keeping your initials, could you? All you did was reverse them. Michael Cantell. Clancy Marshall."

"Your brother," said Ed in disgust. "Your own goddam brother."

"Billy-Billy used to tap him for loans when he was in a bind," I said. "Junky Stein told me how Billy-Billy would go off some place and get money, when he needed it bad enough. But he could only come to the office here. He went at night one time, to Clancy's home, and he didn't get any money." I turned back to

Clancy. "That shook you, that night he came to see you, didn't it, Mike? That wife of yours, you couldn't let her know you had a brother like Billy-Billy Cantell. He was a threat, just like Mavis St. Paul. Not as big a threat, but still a threat. He was a hophead. You can't rely on hopheads, they hit the needle and they talk. When the time came to find a fall guy to replace you in the St. Paul killing, Billy-Billy was the natural choice. Wasn't he, Mike?"

"Listen—" said Clancy. But then he stopped. We were listening, all of us, but he didn't say any more. He stared at us, wide-eyed, looking from one to the other of us, and the block-party smile was gone from his face for good.

"It's true," said Joe Pistol quietly. He looked at me and nodded. "It's true."

Starkweather coughed and got to his feet. "I'd better be leaving," he said. "We can talk about the money situation some other time."

"Call me tomorrow," Ed told him, without looking away from Clancy.

"I will."

Starkweather scurried out, not wanting to know what was going to happen next, and Ed said to Clancy, "You did this. You caused all this trouble. You got the cops down on us and killed your own brother and put the whole goddam organization in a bind. You did it. My own goddam lawyer."

Clancy's mouth moved, but no sound came out of it.

"Okay," said Ed. He got to his feet. "Okay," he said again. "Let's go away from here."

Chapter Twenty-Eight

We went out to the elevator, the five of us, Clancy in the middle. I pushed the button and we waited till the night man brought the elevator up. We boarded, and rode down in silence. I was waiting for Clancy to try something on the way down, but maybe he realized he'd just be killing the old man at the controls if he opened his mouth. Anyway, he kept quiet.

At street level, we followed the night man to the glass doors, and waited while he unlocked one for us. He smiled and nodded and said good night to us, and we all said good night to him, all except Clancy.

We stood on the sidewalk for a few minutes, while Tony Chin went after the car. I stayed close to Clancy, ready for him to make any kind of move at all, either to run or to shout for help, but he stayed nice and quiet all the time.

Ed's Rolls Royce purred up to the curb, and we all climbed in. Joe Pistol sat up front beside Tony Chin, while Ed and Clancy and I sat in back, Clancy in the middle. The car started up, and we drove crosstown.

Clancy swallowed once, loudly, and said, "Ed, I—" but then he stopped again, and he didn't say another word the whole trip.

Tony drove straight over to Ninth and down to the Lincoln Tunnel. I rested a warning hand on Clancy's

knee as we came to the toll booths on the Jersey side
of the tunnel. I felt him tensing, felt him trying to be
brave enough to shout to the guy in the toll booth for
help, but we drove on through with no trouble, and
I felt his body sag again. Hope, as they say, springs
eternal in the coward's breast. Maybe Clancy didn't
really believe his ticket was one-way.

Tony drove along a few of the Jersey roads, and he
obeyed every speed limit there was. We drove on a
four-lane divided highway for a while, and then a three-
laner, and then a bumpy blacktop two-laner, and then
a one-lane dirt road. And then we stopped.

We all got out of the car. It was dark out there, with
the trees and the smell of the Jersey swamps all around
us, the black Rolls behind us, and the only light coming
from a three-quarter moon and a sky full of stars. The
glow over to the east of us was New York. It was hot,
muggy, but none of us noticed it just then.

Ed stood with his back to the car, Tony on his left
and me on his right. Joe Pistol stood near the front of
the car, observing but not a part. Clancy stood wilting,
facing the three of us.

Ed spoke to Clancy then, for the first time since
we'd left the office. "You're going to die out here,
Clancy," he said. "I want you to know why you're
dying. It isn't because you killed the St. Paul woman,
or the Benson woman, or even your brother. It isn't for
killing anybody, killing isn't a crime I worry about.
You're going to die for another crime, far more serious. You're going to die for stupidity. You did a stupid
killing, and you followed it up with two more just as

stupid. You got emotional, you lost your head, and you acted like an amateur. You gave the organization trouble. You used an organization man for a patsy. You acted like an amateur, and I can't have an amateur in the organization."

"Ed," said Clancy. His voice was as faint as the air.

"The killing was a stupid one because it was complicated," Ed told him. "And it was a stupid one because it was emotional. Clancy, we take care of our own, you ought to know that. If you'd come to me about this bitch bothering you, we'd have taken care of it for you. But you got stupid. You took the law into your own hands. *My* law."

"Ed," whispered Clancy.

Ed took a step forward, and we all stood to one side and waited. Ed isn't as young as he used to be, and he's grown accustomed to soft living, but he's still got a hard core inside him. He reached for Clancy, and his left hand grabbed a bunch of shirt front. His right hand came across and clipped Clancy on the side of the jaw. Clancy turned his head, rolling away from the punch, but he didn't roll away from the open back hand that made the return trip.

Tony and Joe and I, we stood to one side, watching and waiting, and Ed worked on Clancy, holding him up with one hand, clubbing him in face and body with the other hand. During the whole thing, nobody said a word, not even Clancy.

Finally, Ed was finished. He backed away from Clancy, lying sprawled on his face in the Jersey mud, and Tony Chin handed him a towel from the glove compartment of the Rolls. Ed wiped his hands on the towel and gave it back to Tony. He was breathing a little hard, but that was all. And his face was completely expressionless.

Tony put the towel back into the car, and then he walked over to me. He pushed out his hand with something in it, and I took it.

It was a Colt .45, one of the blockbusters. I held it in my hand, and looked at it and hefted it. It was the first time I had seen this particular gun, and it would also be the last. After I had finished with it, Tony would take it back and it would disappear. It would cease to exist. Most of the parts would be saved for other guns, but the barrel would be destroyed. The barrel is what they use in ballistics.

I looked over at Ed, and he nodded to me. Then he and Tony and Joe Pistol all walked around to the other side and stood there, looking up at the night sky. It's best to have no witnesses to a thing like this, none at all.

I stepped over in front of Clancy and looked down at him. He was sitting in the mud, half-conscious, propping himself up with one hand. The other hand was wiping at the blood on his face, distractedly.

He was going to die. Because he got trapped by his emotions.

He raised his head, and looked up at me, eyes all white in the darkness, finally believing it, and I turned everything off. I was a machine, and my arm was the arm of the machine, and the gun was a part of the machine. And when the machine's finger contracted, the machine's gun exploded, and that was what the machine was for.

Clancy flipped over backwards, falling awkward and broken, like a puppet when you cut the strings. The machine stepped forward and looked at the broken puppet, and saw that it had been shot in the head, and it wasn't breathing.

Tony Chin came over and dismantled the machine, removing the gun from the hand. I turned around and went back to the Rolls and crawled into the back seat. Tony put the gun somewhere under the front seat, and went back to the body. He picked it up and walked off with it, and Ed got in the back seat with me while Joe Pistol sat up front.

Tony came back a couple minutes later and got two broom-like things out from under the driver's seat. He went around back to attach them to the rear bumper behind the tires. It was a one-lane dirt road, and when we drove back to the two-lane blacktop, we would sweep the dirt road clear of tire tracks.

Once on the blacktop, Tony stopped the car and removed the brooms. Then we drove back to Manhattan

Chapter Twenty-Nine

They let me off in front of my apartment building, and Joe Pistol looked back at me as I was getting out of the car and said, "You're efficient, Clay."

"Thanks," I said.

"You did good work," Ed told me. "Only now I got to get me a new goddam lawyer."

I went upstairs to the apartment. I got myself a beer and sat down in the living room to think. It was eleven o'clock at night. In three hours, I was to pick Ella up at the Tambarin Club, just as I'd been doing every night for almost three weeks now.

But tonight was different from the other nights. Tonight, I had killed a man. All my talk about refusing to maintain the pretty fiction—did I mean I would tell Ella about the killing tonight, and that I would demand she either understand or leave me? If I didn't tell her, I was starting the double life, like Clancy (and look where it got him) and Ed and all the other husbands in this business. If I did tell her, what did I have the right to expect from her?

I could hear the conversation already, three hours before it would happen. She would ask me how I was doing on the case, and I would tell her I'd found the killer. She would ask me who it had turned out to be, and I would tell her, and then she would ask me what had been done about him, and I would say, "Ed beat him up and then I shot him in the head."

And she would want to know why I shot him in the head. And I would have to say, "Because he was stupid." And she would want to know how he had been stupid, and I would have to say, "He gave in to his emotions, and that is stupid."

And I knew what she would say then, too.

Finally, I got to my feet and went out to the bedroom. I got Ella's suitcase out of the closet and packed all her things into it. I carried it down to the parking garage, picked up the Mercedes, and drove to the Tambarin. I walked into the manager's office and gave him the suitcase. I told him to give it to Ella when she finished working that night. "And tell her," I said, "that I said I was sorry."

I left there without easing his curiosity, and drove back home. The Puerto Rican kid at the garage said, "You got any news on the job, mister?"

"You stay right here, you stupid clown," I told him. "It isn't what you think."

I left him gaping at me and went home, where I called Archie Freihofer. "Archie," I said, "I want you to send me a girl. Right now. Any girl, I don't care who. Just so she's somebody I won't be sorry to say goodbye to in the morning."

While I waited, I thought again about the killing, and about the impossibility of describing the necessity of it to Ella. That a business necessity is—

Then I stopped in my tracks, and took a good close look at the killing I'd just done. Business? We didn't make a penny when we killed Clancy Marshall. We didn't save a penny. We didn't remove any legal heat; that was removed when Billy-Billy's body was found by the cops.

There was no business reason to kill Clancy Marshall.

But *I* had been emotionless.

But Ed had beaten him up. Ed had been emotional. *Ed* had been emotional. Ed had been *emotional*.

Clancy Marshall. Not Billy-Billy Cantell, not some two-bit hood the cops would be glad to see dead. Clancy Marshall, a lawyer, a man with a wife and two kids, a man with a respectable front. The cops would investigate, they would have to investigate. They would dig and dig, and it wouldn't take them long—

I ran to the phone. Ed was home. "His office, Ed," I said. "We've got to clean out the office."

"Good thinking, boy," he said. He didn't seem bothered about that at all. "It's being taken care of, I already thought of it. Don't you worry about a thing."

"What about the wife, his wife?"

"She stayed out of the business, Clay, you know that. Don't worry."

"Sure," I said, and hung up.

But I kept thinking about the wife. She'd seen me, she'd seen me last night at one o'clock. The cops would talk to her and she'd say yes, there was a strange man here last night, at one o'clock. And they would show her pictures.

We had to set somebody up. We couldn't leave it unexplained, they'd dig and dig and they'd find *me*. We had to set it up for them, give them a fall guy.

I reached for the phone again, but my hand stopped before touching it. I remembered Ed's last words about Clancy Marshall. "Now I got to get me a new goddam lawyer." As easy as that.

He had the gun!

But he couldn't throw me away, I was his boy, his good right hand. Damn it, I knew too much for him to throw me away.

The thoughts streamed this way, that way, flowing and flooding, and the doorbell sounded.

It would be the girl Archie was supposed to send over. Of course. Who else would be coming here? It would be the girl Archie was supposed to send over.

It rang again.

Get Hard Case Crime by Mail...
And Save 43%!

☐ YES! Sign me up for the Hard Case Crime Book Club!

As long as I choose to stay in the club, I will receive every Hard Case Crime book as it is published (generally one each month). I'll get to preview each title for 10 days. If I decide to keep it, I will pay only $3.99* — a savings of 43% off the cover price! There is no minimum number of books I must buy and I may cancel my membership at any time.

Name: _____

Address: _____

City / State / ZIP: _____

Telephone: _____

E-Mail: _____

☐ I want to pay by credit card: ☐ VISA ☐ MasterCard ☐ Discover

Card #: _____ Exp. date: _____

Signature: _____

Mail this page to:

HARD CASE CRIME BOOK CLUB
20 Academy Street, Norwalk, CT 06850-4032

Or fax it to 610-995-9274.
You can also sign up online at www.dorchesterpub.com.

* Plus $2.00 for shipping. Offer open to residents of the U.S. and Canada only. Canadian residents please call 1-800-481-9191 for pricing information.

If you are under 18, a parent or guardian must sign. Terms, prices, and conditions subject to change. Subscription subject to acceptance. Dorchester Publishing reserves the right to reject any order or cancel any subscription.